MW00737734

Day of the Hired Gun

Hired gunfighter Cole Jardine has decided to call time on his dangerous profession when he receives a mysterious job offer from the Colorado town of Red Mesa. All set to ignore it, his partner Waco Santee suddenly arrives back at their cabin in Wyoming to announce that the army are hot on their heels. With minutes to spare, flight across the border is their only option. The pair succeed in evading pursuit and then head their separate ways.

But nothing is ever that simple. A bushwhacker attempts to remove Cole but fails. Arriving in Red Mesa, he is then challenged to a shoot-out by rancher Ed Clifford who claims the gunslinger has been hired by an unscrupulous crook who wants to steal his land. Which faction will the hired gun support? And how will he react when his old partner turns up backing the opposing side in the dispute?

Day of the Hired Gun

Ethan Flagg

A Black Horse Western

ROBERT HALE

© Ethan Flagg 2017
First published in Great Britain 2017

ISBN 978-0-7198-2399-2

The Crowood Press
The Stable Block
Crowood Lane
Ramsbury
Marlborough
Wiltshire SN8 2HR

www.bhwesterns.com

Robert Hale is an imprint
of The Crowood Press

Typeset by
Derek Doyle & Associates, Shaw Heath
Printed and bound in Great Britain by
CPI Group (UK) Ltd, Croydon, CR0 4YY

AUTHOR'S NOTE

In the early days of the American West, the term 'wild' was a fair reflection of frontier territories where law and order was in its infancy. Those officers appointed to administer justice had to oversee large areas which often proved impossible to cover effectively. Especially after the Civil War, many combatants released from service found it difficult to settle down. Numerous ruthless gangs evolved, all eager to take advantage of the free rein offered.

To combat their depredations, vigilance committees were formed by citizens desperate for stability. Punishment of apprehended felons was accordingly often swift and brutal, such action being sanctioned by kangaroo courts. The carrying out of these on-the-spot responses was intended to send a clear message to those intent on causing mayhem.

The gap between anarchy and vigilante law was filled by skilled manipulators in the deadly art of triggernometry. These hired gunslingers considered themselves a cut above the vigilante groups formed to bring order to territory where no official law existed. Reputations were earned by undertaking paid work where the use of firearms was deemed essential. Unlike bounty hunters who used their shooting skill to bring in wanted felons for a prescribed reward, the hired gunman generally worked for a set fee. Men of wealth seeking to protect their own private interests had little trouble in hiring such mercenaries.

As a group, hired gunmen worked as much within the law as outside it, carrying out a pre-arranged job before disappearing into the wild blue yonder from whence they had emerged. Many had already pursued careers as bandits or lawmen, often both. Few had any qualms about working on either side of the legal divide. So long as the pay was right, they would accept any task considered within their capabilities.

There was no shortage of employers willing to pay large sums to hard-boiled jaspers who displayed no compunction in using their six shooters to achieve a satisfactory conclusion. Overland stage companies hired freelance guards to prevent harassment from road agents. The railroads likewise took on private detectives to combat the depredations of train robbers such as the Reno Brothers and James Gang. So-called 'railroad inspectors' were given carte blanche to protect the companies' interests where the regular law enforcement agencies proved inadequate.

Many hired gunmen worked for the large cattle spreads ranging from Texas to Montana. Their job was to beat off the encroachment of the dreaded sheepherders and homesteaders. The former were accused of destroying valuable grazing land while the latter encouraged the use of barbed wire to section off the much-revered open range. Most common though, was the problem caused by cattle thieves. Regular cowboys refused to challenge the rustler gangs, asserting they were not paid to fight, but to manage beef on the hoof.

Wealthy landowners accordingly often employed hard-nosed mercenaries who were given official titles such as 'cattle detectives' or 'stock inspectors'. Friction between cowboys and shootists was inevitable and often led to fights. When rustlers were caught, a necktie party was the usual method of encouraging other such villains to think twice before embarking on their larcenous activities. Should the hired operatives be apprehended by official lawmen, they could always rely on employers to get them off the hook by means of bribery or the machinations of shifty and equally well-paid lawyers. But these cases were the exception.

Most of these men preferred to remain nameless, flitting about like wraiths on the wind. One month here, another there. As such they were well nigh impossible to pin down by the established law enforcement authorities. And therein lay their success. They operated not so much in defiance of the law as beyond its reach. Most abhorred any form of notoriety, leaving little personal trace of their deadly labours.

7

Yet some were so successful at their work, a reputation was impossible to avoid. Names were passed down the grapevine when a reliable gun hand was required. Men like these could command the highest fees, literally naming their own price. There was also the added bonus of securing bounties when wanted outlaws were apprehended. Their names shone bright in contrast to the grey anonymity of the average hired gun.

Such a man was Cole Jardine. . . .

ONE

SUDDEN DEPARTURE

For the third time in as many minutes, the granite-hard face of Cole Jardine perused the letter he had picked up in Rock Springs that morning. The message was brisk and to the point – *Well paid job in Red Mesa, Colorado. Bring your guns.* It was signed 'Kez Randle'. No mention of what the job entailed. Cole frowned. His craggy features puckered up in disdain. He and his partner, Waco Santee, were doing well in Wyoming. They had signed up to organize a threatened takeover bid of the cattle outfit run by wealthy landowner Mason Treherne.

The altercation between Treherne's Triple X brand and the Rising Sun had escalated into a full-blown range war. Each of the opposing factions wanted to be top dog in the Sweetwater Valley and neither was willing to compromise. Not that Cole and his buddy were complaining. As long as the generous fees kept being paid into their bank accounts, they would continue to back the winning side. And that was the Triple X.

The last couple of days had seen a lull in the violence. Cole had welcomed the opportunity to enjoy some fun in the county seat at Rock Springs. His pard had taken a shine to one of the girls working in the Flaming Gorge saloon. Waco had promised to be back in time for a noon meeting with Treherne to discuss future tactics.

Once again, Cole looked at the message. Known throughout the western territories as Kingpin, he had earned the nickname on account of the pledge stated on his business card to 'Go anywhere! Do anything!' The slogan, written across the leading royal chess piece, was not quite a true claim, however. Cole would only take on jobs of which he approved. He was one of the few hired guns who could honestly claim to have scruples.

The number of desperadoes to have fallen victim to his deadly accuracy with a six-shooter was now well into double figures. According to the straight-faced mercenary, every last one of the critters had warranted their abrupt departure from this mortal coil.

In the current situation, he was backing Mason Treherne due to a belief that he was in the right. Jake Logan of the Rising Sun had been rustling his stock. A particularly fierce confrontation had taken place with Logan's own hired gunnies led by a rival called

Black Matt Sangster the previous week. Waco had accounted for two of Sangster's men with his Henry repeater. The others were now being held for trial in the Rock Springs jailhouse. But the gang leader himself had managed to slip the net.

Sipping his coffee Cole replayed the chase that had followed when the black-hearted gunman realized he had met his match in Cole Jardine. But Sangster was not about to surrender without a fight. 'You'll never take me alive, Kingpin,' he called out from behind some boulders where he was the last man standing.

'I don't need to, buster,' Cole replied. 'You're worth a cool thousand, dead or alive. Reckon though I'd prefer taking you in slung over a saddle.'

The next thing he heard was the pounding of hoofs as Black Matt made his bid for freedom. Cole was not slow in following. In and out of the rocky enclaves the chase went, finally terminating in a box canyon. Black Matt cursed aloud knowing he had made a big mistake. Too late for regrets now.

He ditched his cayuse, scuttling up the loose scree to hide amidst the plethora of craggy recesses. A cliff face soared high above where the hired gunman finished up. So steep was this end of the box canyon even a mountain goat would have balked at making the climb.

And there he made his stand, pumping out a couple of bullets that brought down Cole's horse. Leaping off the fallen roan, the pursuer scrambled behind some rocks. Numerous shots were exchanged with little effect on either party. A neutral stand-off

11

had unwittingly been occasioned, a war of attrition with neither man likely to gain the ascendancy. Nobody was going anywhere fast.

Being a guy not noted for his patience, Cole was eager to get this over with in double-quick time. Accordingly he resorted to an old decoy trick to which no level-headed gunslinger would ever have succumbed. His hat was laid on a rock with the Winchester poking out of a notch. Then he crawled across to his left silently willing the fugitive to holler out the inevitable shout of exhilaration. But would the varmint fall for such an old chestnut recreated in numerous dime Western tales?

Three shots rang out, the sharp reports bouncing off the bare rock walls. 'Got the bastard,' came the gleeful cry of triumph. Sangster clearly didn't read novels. Moments later, the gunman appeared, stealthily wending his way down to where he expected to find the corpse of his adversary. Shock was written across the grizzled countenance when the awful truth dawned. 'Never figured a smart jasper like you would fall for that old trick,' Cole dispassionately remarked, holding his gun steady while covering the outlaw. 'Make it easy for us both and drop the gun, Matt.'

Sangster snarled as he slowly dropped his gun back into the holster. 'I've always had a hankering to take over as Kingpin of the hired guns. How about you proving the great Cole Jardine still has what it takes?'

It was a clear challenge that Cole's pride demanded he accept. All the same, he kept a hawkish eye on his opponent while settling into position. It looked as though for once, Black Matt Sangster was going play by the rules.

The two men faced each other. It was Cole who suggested the way forward, or not as the case may be for one of them. He pointed to an eagle floating on the thermals overhead. The bird was clearly looking for its dinner. 'Soon as that guy hooks up his prey we start to shooting. Agreed?' Sangster nodded as both men avidly followed the bird's hunting instincts.

Minutes passed. Then suddenly the bird dropped. Down, down, down it fell, its talons latching onto a desert rat. And that's when all hell broke loose in that remote canyon. The yammer of black powder shells tore bloody holes in the tense silence. Half a dozen shots were fired before Matt Sangster staggered back, a hand clutching at the fatal wound in his chest. Cole did not escape unhurt. But it was only a flesh wound in the leg.

A satisfied half smile lingered on Cole's face as he finished his coffee and hooked out a pocket watch. Time was getting on. Waco should have been here by now. That guy couldn't keep his hands off the dames. But Cole wasn't worried. His pard was always solidly dependable. He would be along in time for the meeting.

Although only two in number, Kingpin Jardine and his buddy had proved their worth to the rancher. The sixth sense possessed by the hired gunfighter with regard to countering opposition tactics was second to none. Treherne had not quibbled at the high fee demanded. You want the best, you pay for it. And such had proved to be the case with the removal of the infamous Black Matt.

Jake Logan had not taken kindly to the beating. A couple of line cabins had been burnt to the ground. Luckily they were empty at the time. A Texan through and through, the irate rancher had threatened to bring in a bunch of what he called 'real' gunslingers from the Brazos country. Things were really hotting up in the Sweetwater Basin. The current period of strained respite felt like the calm before the storm.

Now in his mid thirties, Cole knew that he was well past his prime in this line of work. Sure he was still the Kingpin, but the life of a hired gunman rarely passed beyond the thirty mark. It was definitely a young man's game. He was on borrowed time, and knew it. Sooner or later, a bullet was going to find its way into his hide and stay there. After this current job was over, he promised himself to settle down and buy that ranch he had always wanted. Perhaps even find himself a wife to keep him warm at night.

With that thought in mind, Cole was about to toss the recent message into the fireplace when the door of the line cabin burst open. In the flash of a rattler's strike, the nickel-plated Colt .45 jumped into his hand. No loss of reflexes could be detected when the chips were down. At the same time he threw himself behind a solid oak chest. Nevertheless, he could well do without such a strain on his ticker which was belting out a frenetic drum roll.

It eased back to a steady thud on recognizing the bulky silhouette of his pard standing in the open doorway. 'Goldarn it, Waco!' the Kingpin robustly berated his pal while scrambling to his feet. 'You trying to give me a heart attack?'

Santee ignored the protest. 'Grab your gear, pal, and let's get out of here double quick.' His earnest command laced with a raw measure of alarm saw the burly Santee quickly assembling his own meagre possessions. Before Cole could express any enquires about this sudden announcement, Waco poured out the reason for his panic-stricken haste. 'The governor is so all-fired up about this range war, he's called in the army to squash it. And guess who they have in their sights?'

It was clear from his buddy's rapid-fire elucidation that the bluecoats were hot on his heels. 'How much time do we have?' Cole snapped out, lurching to his feet.

'They'll be here in ten minutes at most. So we need to hit the trail pronto.'

No more time was wasted on futile chinwagging. Men in their line of work travelled light of necessity for just such an eventuality as this. In five minutes, they were in the saddle and heading south. Cole's intention was to lose their pursuers in the foothills of the Divide.

And they were only just in time. A plume of dust heralded the imminent arrival of the cavalry. They could even hear the heavy pounding of hoof beats indicating a large force was in pursuit. Spurs dug deep as the two riders urged their horses to the gallop. It was essential to reach the distant pine and aspen trees for the cover they afforded. Five miles of open plain had to be crossed before they could hope to evade their pursuers.

Halfway to the distant line of trees marking the start of higher ground, it was clear that the boys in blue were gaining. Cole shouted out, his voice straining to override the ear-crunching thud of shod hoofs. 'We'll never outrun these guys at this pace.'

'What do you have in mind, pal?' came back the edgy reply.

'Soon as we pass over that next ridge up ahead, there's a couple of sandstone pinnacles on each side of the trail. Remember?' Waco nodded. 'Swerve off behind them. Soon as the soldier boys have passed, we'll take the old Indian trail over the Divide down to the border at Ladore Falls. That should fool them.'

Concentrating on reaching the Needles in time, and without being spotted, each man gritted his teeth and prayed for deliverance. Bodies low and stretched out to secure the maximum speed from tiring horses, they ploughed onward towards the two landmarks that had come into view. A quick glance behind informed Cole that reaching the Needles without being spotted would be touch and go.

They made it with a couple of minutes to spare. Concealed behind the towering buttes, the two men held their breath as the line of horse soldiers thundered past without the slightest hesitation on their part. The two fugitives grinned at one another. 'We did it, buddy,' an elated Cole Jardine gushed. 'Let's eat dust before those mugs twig they've been fooled.'

16

'Reminds me of that time in the Black Hills when Ike Banner took exception to us ruining his claim jumping scam,' Waco enthused to wild chuckles from his pard. 'Boy, was he mad.'

'Never caught us though,' added Cole. 'And neither will those blue bellies.' And with that he spurred off along the hidden trail.

Ten minutes later it was clear to both men that they had managed to elude their pursuers. They slowed to a gentle canter as the narrow trail meandered through the surging buttresses of rock. Waco was impressed. 'Them Shoshone braves sure have a sixth sense when it comes to sniffing out the best route through these mountains.'

His partner was no less admiring of the canny knack displayed by the native tribesmen. 'They've been living here a sight longer than the white man. I sometimes reckon we have a nerve muscling in on their homeland. You can't rightly blame them for fighting back.'

They were now high into the mountains and forced to don fleece-lined jackets to combat the cold. Even though it was mid summer, the high peaks still retained their capping of snow all year through. Two more days passed before the zenith was reached at a gap known as The Devil's Reach.

After crossing the Divide separating the country's east and west river systems, the two buddies dropped steadily down through the ruggedly beautiful terrain of the Rocky Mountains. Heading in a general southerly direction the only person they encountered was a grizzled mountain man trapping beaver. They stayed in the old timer's log cabin overnight enjoying a mite too much power-packed moonshine. But at least they slept well.

Later the next day they finally emerged from the enclosing confines of the tree clad slopes where Muddy Creek tumbled down through the crashing cascade of the Ladore Falls into a wide plain below. Cole pointed to a huddle of shacks looking remarkably like a miniature toy town. 'That place down yonder is called Baggs,' he said. 'On the far side of the creek is Colorado. Guess this is where we part company.' It was a poignant moment that both men knew was coming, yet were somehow loathe to acknowledge. They had been together four years. 'Where you headed, pal?'

'Figured I go east into the Medicine Bow country,' Waco replied.

'What's so interesting up there?'

'Sheep.'

Cole eyed his buddy askance. 'Sheep!' he exclaimed somewhat sceptically. 'Sounds too much like trouble to me.'

'That's what it's all about, ain't it?' Waco shrugged. 'The ranchers up there are offering good money to keep those woollies backs off'n their land. Sure I can't persuade you to tag along?'

Cole shook his head. 'Reckon I'll check out that job in Red Mesa. See what it involves and how much they're offering.'

'You still after going into retirement on that spread

18

you've been talking about?' Waco scoffed good-naturedly. 'I'd say it sounds a tad on the dull side for a guy of the Kingpin's reputation.'

'A fella has to settle down sometime if'n he wants to keep breathing. You never thought about it?'

Waco considered the question. 'I did once.' He paused, noting his buddy's interest. A wry smirk coated his dark stubbly features. 'Lucky for me that dozy sheriff forgot to lock the cell door and I escaped.'

Both men chuckled uproariously. Then Cole reluctantly held out a hand. 'Well, this is it, the parting of the ways. Good luck to you, old buddy. Be seeing you around.' Their eyes met as firm hands were clasped.

'You take care, pal,' Waco cautioned, a serious expression now replacing the light-hearted banter. 'That rep you've earned ain't no idle daydream. There's plenty guys out there would love nothing more than to be the desperado who took down the Kingpin.'

Cole nodded his understanding. He knew the score. No more words were spoken. None were needed. He nudged his horse down the steeply winding track leading down to Baggs, while his pal continued along the ridge. Neither looked back. Destiny had made its choice and would determine whatever the future had in store.

TWO

BUSHWHACKED

Two days into Colorado, Cole was idly speculating on the mysterious letter from the equally vague Kez Randle when his thoughts were brutally cut short. The loud throaty discharge of a heavy-gauge long gun shattered the tranquil silence. Three times the gun roared. Cole was thrown to the ground. His horse had taken one of the bullets in the neck. The shots had come from behind. Luckily the others missed their premeditated target. This jasper was no professional killer; that was for sure. Any sniper worthy of the name would have taken him out with the first shot.

The proposed victim rolled behind the dead carcass and whipped his carbine out of the saddle boot. Three rapid-fire shots were levered off towards the plume of smoke rising from a cluster of rocks higher up on his left. No further reply was forthcoming from the hidden bushwhacker. Having failed in his devious mission, the varmint appeared to have slunk away.

Cole waited five minutes before gingerly emerging from cover. Rifle at the ready he circled around, edging up towards where the gunman had been waiting. And there behind a large boulder, he discovered a cluster of empty brass cartridge cases. They were large calibre. He stuck them in the pocket of his buckskin jacket.

Judging by the ashes of a fire, and an abandoned coffee pot, it appeared this guy had been here for some time. A menacing scowl cloaked the Kingpin's craggy face. It was clear he had been expected. Could this have something to do with the job in Red Mesa? It sure looked that way. Somebody clearly didn't want him around.

Now cast afoot, Cole returned to his horse and removed the saddle and tack, heaving it up onto his shoulders. It would be a long walk to his destination. Not the sort of trek for a guy wearing riding boots. Luckily, he soon dropped down through the rough terrain onto a main highway. And there he waited hoping that some form of transport would happen along. An hour later a stagecoach rumbled to a halt.

The driver eyed the unusual sight of a man carrying his saddle. 'Your horse get fed up, did he?' the guy commented, maintaining a solemn regard. 'Lumbered you with his saddle?'

Cole nodded. 'I carried him most of the way until

21

he found some other poor sucker to do the job,' he replied with equal gravity, fully appreciating the teamster's dry wit.

The driver pondered awhile before replying. 'Had the same trouble myself once. A team of four refused to pull this coach. I had to stick them lazy nags inside and haul the darn coach myself. You after a ride, mister?'

'Figure that's the easiest way to reach Red Mesa. Only if'n you have room though. No horses this trip I hope.' He handed his rig up to the driver who lumped it onto the roof with the other baggage.

'Just human passengers fortunately. They tend to smell better.'

'My intrusion might alter that state of affairs seeing as I ain't partaken of a bath in a dog's age.'

A languid eye panned across the buckskin-clad figure. It was followed by a twitchy sniff. 'You smell a sight better'n them nags. Hop inside. I'm behind schedule already. That Overland manager in Mesa will be stewing in his juice if'n I'm late.'

There were two other passengers. Cole was given no chance to sit down as the driver whipped up the team with a hearty whoop. He fell into the lap of a young woman who was none too pleased at the unexpected intrusion. Cole just sat there ogling this highly delectable travelling companion.

'Would you mind please,' the girl snorted, trying ineffectually to distance herself from this smelly interloper.

'I don't mind in the least,' Cole replied, quite

22

happy to remain where he was. 'but only if'n you don't.' His admiring gaze caressed the smoothly sculpted features, the swan-like neck. Even the silly hat perched atop a pinned-up coiffure of auburn tresses did not detract from the dreamy apparition.

Had this unusual introduction been with a more earthy dame, such as a saloon gal with whom he was more familiar, the handsome stranger would doubt-less have received a more cordial reaction. But Eleanor Clifford was unimpressed by the slick patter and easy-going charm. And the rank odour oozing from those buckskin duds that tended not to be washed in order to preserve their waterproofing qual-ities sure didn't help his case.

Her nose wrinkled disdainfully. 'Well I certainly do. This seat has been paid for. And I have no intentions of sharing it. Take the one next to that gentleman. And be quick about it.'

The young woman's imperious tone in no way fazed the newcomer. He tipped his hat acknowledg-ing her curt wishes and sat down opposite. Only then did he notice the other passenger. A seedy looking jasper in a check suit immediately placed him in the category of a travelling drummer. The valise on the floor had to contain his samples. The guy's shifty gaze fastened onto their recent addition.

'Don't I know you from somewhere, sir?' the man enquired thoughtfully, rubbing his jutting chin. 'Hyram Tranter never forgets a face.' The drummer's brow crinkled in thought.

Cole reluctantly dragged his eyes away from the far

more alluring passenger. 'I've been around some,' was the blunt response intended to squash any further prying as he turned his attention back to the girl.

But Tranter was not to be deflected. His beady eyes widened, a finger pointed, the thin-lipped mouth opening as recognition dawned. 'You're Cole Jardine. I saw your picture splashed across the front page of the *Wyoming Sentinel*. They call you the Kingpin on account of. . . .' The animated declaration faded to a sibilant mutter, occasioned by the menacing glare that skewered the drummer to his seat. The guy's face blanched nervously as he drew back.

No denial as to the validity of the drummer's claim, nor any admission was forthcoming. Only a flat retort chock full of menace. 'Fellas that point the finger run the risk of having it chopped off, mister. You'd do well to pay more attention to your samples. It'll be a sight more healthy.'

'M-maybe I was a bit h-hasty,' Tranter stuttered, gulping nervously. 'Now I come to think of it, you look n-nothing like the Kingpin.' And with that the little guy hunkered down into his seat and kept quiet.

Much as Cole tried to engage the stunning Miss Clifford in conversation, all he received back were monosyllabic rejoinders. He soon gave up. The rest of the journey was conducted in silence. Some enlivenment was provided by the tuneful renditions of the latest ditties from Whiplash the driver. If only second choice, the ever-changing countryside offered an interesting distraction in the form of jack rabbits and deer darting across the trail. The driver took regular pot shots at them with his rifle, none of which found their mark.

THREE

RED MESA

It was, therefore, with some degree of relief for all concerned when the coach arrived at Red Mesa two hours later. The town lay on the edge of a broad flat plain of rich grassland watered by the mighty Gunnison River. It was ideal country for raising beef cattle. And judging by the bustling nature of the town it was prospering. Cole peered out of the window, noticing the main street had nightlights. There was even a guy employed to clean up dung deposited by the large number of horse-drawn wagons plying up and down. Clearly there was money to be made here.

A call from the driver up top heralded their arrival with a jaunty, 'Red Mesa, folks. End of the line. And only half an hour late. Enjoy your stay.' The coach rumbled to a halt outside the Overland Depot to be greeted by the local agent.

'You're late, Whiplash,' Elver Wickes grumbled

checking his watch. 'You stopped off at Shorty Juke's Trading Post again for a quick snort, didn't yuh?' the pedantic agent called up to the driver.

'Now that's where you're wrong, Mr Wickes,' Whiplash hotly denied. 'I did my duty as a big-hearted employee of the company by stopping to pick up a stranded traveller. Ain't that the case, mister?'

Before Cole could agree, the sweating figure of Hyram Tranter flung open the coach door and jumped down. The nervous drummer hurried off, thankful to distance himself from the renowned gun-slinger still inside the coach. 'Something must have spooked him,' declared a puzzled Wickes, scratching his head. 'You ain't been driving too fast I hope, Whiplash.'

The driver scoffed at the notion as he unloaded the baggage. Cole was next out so as to help the lady down. She purposely ignored the proffered hand. 'I can manage quite well without your help, thank you,' she snorted loftily, not even bothering to acknowledge the gesture. A dainty lace handkerchief wafted away the unsightly odour of tanned animal skin.

'Guess I'll have to get me a change of clothes and a bath for the next time we meet, ma'am,' Cole said.

'Somehow I can't see that happening,' Miss Clifford replied, turning her attention to the agent. 'Have my bags sent over to the Drover's Cottage, please.'

'With pleasure, ma'am,' the agent said with a crisp bow while gesturing to a hovering lackey. Then turning to the sole remaining passenger, he added with a sly grin, 'That gal don't seem to like you, mister.'

Cole smiled. 'Maybe that's 'cos she don't know me well enough. I tend to grow on folks . . . if'n they'll let me, that is.' And with that he wandered across to the more basic National Hotel.

Appreciative eyes followed the girl as she sauntered across to the hotel/meeting place specially reserved for ranchers and their crews. But this was no shrinking violet of a building. Resplendent upper floors of the Cottage housed sumptuous accommodation, restaurant and gaming rooms for the more prosperous landowners. Smaller outfits and cowhands made do with an annex built onto the rear. Nowhere near as snazzy. But vastly reduced rates made it a popular place to spend their days off.

Cole Jardine was not the only one admiring the sleek cat-like progression down the main street. A lean-limbed jasper clad in range garb watched from an upper window. Dan Mather's lip curled irritably on witnessing the buckskinned passenger according rather too much attention to the girl; his girl. The jealous suitor held his simmering anger in check to address his older associate.

Ed Clifford ran the Flying C ranch and Mather was his foreman. The two men were on tenterhooks awaiting the arrival of Clifford's daughter who had been despatched on a begging mission to the Western Credit and Finance Company in Grand Junction. 'Eleanor's back,' Mather announced. 'We'll soon find out if'n she's managed to persuade those tight-fisted critters to give us the loan we need.'

A few minutes later Eleanor Clifford entered the room. It was clear from her downcast expression that the trip had not been a success. 'I did my best, Dad,' she murmured, removing the poky hat. 'But they reckon we're a bad risk.'

The rancher accepted the news philosophically. 'I didn't think they would, knowing the ranch is in such bad straits. But it was worth a try.' Eleanor hugged her disconsolate father, feeling the anguish throbbing inside his chest.

'Don't I get a hug?' Mather butted in, breaking the heartfelt moment.

'Sorry, Dan. I didn't see you over there.' She offered her cheek for a brief kiss. Then turned her attention back to the older man. 'I think we should get back to the ranch right away,' she postulated hurriedly. 'There's no reason now for hanging around Red Mesa.'

'But you've only just arrived back, honey,' her father protested. 'Why not freshen up and stay here tonight? Plenty of time to head back in the morning. I'm sure the tight budget we're on will run to a decent meal in the Cottage.' He turned to address his foreman. 'How long do you figure it'll take to drive that herd to Fort Belvedere, Dan? Looks like we ain't got no choice now the chips are down.'

'Reckon about a week to round all them steers up, then another two weeks on the trail,' came back the snappy response. 'That should give us enough time to pay off that loan you borrowed from Kez Randle.'

Clifford stamped about the room berating himself. 'I ought never to have trusted that varmint. He gave us three months to pay it back then welched on the deal claiming I should have read the contract properly. The rat knew all along that we couldn't drive them beeves to the northern railhead at South Pass in the four weeks he's given us to pay up.'

'Lucky for us that new fort the army is building at Belvedere is ready for occupation,' Mather enthused. 'They're paying top dollar for good stock. And we'll have spare dough to build up the spread again.'

Eleanor was not listening. She had another, in her view, far more serious issue troubling her. The girl's anxious plea, the wringing of hands, was instantly picked up by her father. 'Something else bothering you, Eleanor?' The girl hesitated. 'Come on, girl. Best spit it out.'

She swallowed nervously before delivering the bad news. 'Cole Jardine is in town. He joined the stage up by Aspen Draw. Claimed some bushwhacker had shot his horse from under him.'

'Did he see who did it?' Mather asked somewhat edgily.

Eleanor shook her head, unaware of the foreman's nervous reaction. 'What's a hired gunman like that doing in Red Mesa?'

'I certainly know the answer to that,' interjected Clifford, his thick grey moustache bristling with indignation. 'Randle must have sent for him. The rat figures if'n Jardine rubs me out, he'll have a heap less hassle taking over the Flying C.'

'And that will mean he owns all the land at that end of the valley,' added Mather. 'I know Randle's a land-grabbing skunk. But why only the north end?'

'The Union Pacific is planning on building an extension down this way. Anyone who owns all that land will make a big profit from the sale.'

Once again, Eleanor pleaded with her father to leave town. But to no avail.

'I'd do anything you ask, sweetheart. You know that don't you?' The girl responded with a perfunctory nod. 'Except for this one thing. A man has his pride. And that includes protecting his honour as well as his assets.' The rancher lifted his revolver out of the holster and checked the load. He spun the chambers and slotted the gun back, settling it on his hip. 'I built this ranch up with my own hands through good times and bad. Your mother, God rest her soul, was by my side all the way.' His voice hardened alongside the look of grim determination. 'And no tinpot gun-slinger is gonna force me out.'

'I'll come down with you, Ed,' the foreman averred. 'We'll face him together.'

'No, Dan. This is my problem and I'll sort it.' Then he gently moved his daughter aside and reached for the door handle. 'Look after Eleanor. Whatever happens down there, I need to know she'll be taken care of.'

'You can count on me,' the foreman promised, laying an arm around the girl's trembling shoulders.

'Men!' the distraught girl cried out, shaking him off. 'You're all the same. Too darned stubborn for

31

your own good.' She turned away, head in hands, as her father left the room heading for a fate that was now in the lap of the gods.

FOUR

CALLED OUT

As Cole sauntered across to the National Hotel, his progress was followed by numerous other pairs of curious eyes. Hyram Tranter had been quick to inform all within earshot about the arrival of the notorious hired gunslinger in Red Mesa. The man under scrutiny paid no heed, being well used to folks giving him a wide berth. He entered the hotel lobby where a surly jasper barred his way. The guy introduced himself as Rube Thurman, one of Kez Randle's henchmen.

A six gun was immediately brandished under the guy's bulbous snout. 'Bit twitchy, ain't you, Kingpin,' the guy complained, nevertheless holding his arms well clear of the holstered six shooter.

'I been shot at once already today,' was the brusque rejoinder. 'So I ain't taking no chances. You want something then spit it out.'

'The boss wants you round at the Yellow Dog saloon for a pow-wow as soon as you've settled in,' Thurman rapped out. 'And he don't like to be kept waiting.'

'That so,' rasped the clearly irked newcomer. 'You tell Kez Randle that I'll be along to see him in my own good time.'

'He ain't gonna like that,' replied the confused lackey, who was more used to having orders obeyed without comment.

'That's his problem. Now cut along, mister, while I suss out this town.' Cole turned his back on the minder and ambled across to sign in at the hotel reception.

'I'll take a room overlooking the main street,' he said to a decidedly nervous clerk.

The guy was sweating buckets. The arrival in Red Mesa of a name boasting such an infamous repute as Cole Jardine's had clearly spread like a flash flood. He smiled to himself. 'Don't you think a man of your standing, Mr Jardine, would prefer a room at the Drover's Cottage?' Cole raised a questioning eyebrow. 'It's much more comfortable than the National, and . . .' the poor guy hesitated, a nervous finger loosening his tight collar, '. . . and our rooms have mice.'

Cole held his hand out for the key. His face remained inscrutable as he replied, 'You can rely on me not to bother them.'

With some reluctance the key was passed across. 'Number sixteen on the first floor. Have a nice stay, sir.' In a much quieter voice, the clerk offered up an earnest prayer that it would be a brief one.

Ten minutes later, Cole strolled out of the hotel and made his way across the street. He wanted to find out what calibre of bullet had been used in the bush-whacking. He was halfway across when a gruff yet measured voice hailed him from behind. 'If'n you're looking for me, Kingpin, no need to search any further.'

Cole slowly turned around. An old grizzled guy well into his fifties but with an upright and resolute bearing stood close by in readiness for a showdown. His hand was hovering above a low-slung gun belt. He gave the impression he had done this before. But that was clearly a long time in the past. And in Cole's con-sidered view, a guy wearing spectacles ought to stay home tending his vegetable plot.

'Am I supposed to know you, mister?' Cole asked.

'Don't come the funny stuff with me, Jardine,' the guy snapped back. 'Everyone in town knows why you're here. Kez Randle has made sure of that. So let's get to it.'

Cole frowned. 'A pity I don't know what you're talking about.' He was genuinely puzzled. 'Maybe you should spill the beans. I always have a hankering to know who it is I'm supposed to be taking out.'

The challenger was becoming irritated at this guy's nonchalant manner. 'Don't play the innocent with me, Jardine. You know full well why Randle sent for you. The rat obviously wants me out of his hair. The name is Ed Clifford by the way. I run the Flying C ranch, as if you didn't know.' The light was beginning to dawn in Cole's confused mind. So this was what that note was all about. 'My advice to you, Jardine, is to be on the next stage leaving town.'

'And what if'n I don't want to leave?'

'Then we settle this right here and now.' Clifford hunched down, his right hand twitching above the butt of his revolver.

Cole couldn't help noticing that it was a Cooper double-action .36 navy model. Not one of the latest firearms. This guy clearly was no gunfighter. A host of the idly curious, along with the shocked and disturbed, watched from a safe distance. A bird chirruped before conforming to the stiff silence. All were ignored by both participants in this age-old ritual of settling disputes.

The old timer certainly had guts, Cole surmised, his hawkish gaze studying the rancher's every movement. He tried one last time to calm the guy down. 'I ain't got no beef with you, mister. What say we talk this over before things get out of hand?'

The entreaty fell upon deaf ears. Clifford was beyond the point of no return. 'Quit jawing and fill your hand or crawl away, big shot!' The growled response found the challenger clawing for his gun. He did manage to draw and raise the old Cooper. But no further. Cole's bullet ripped it from his grasp, the chunk of hot lead scoring a furrow across his hand. Clifford's face creased in pain as he dropped to one knee clutching at the injured appendage.

Cole walked up to the beaten adversary and stood over him. Then quickly reached down and palmed

36

the fallen pistol. No sense putting ideas into the guy's head about trying to finish the job with his good hand. 'That was a stupid move, mister. I could have killed you.'

'Then why didn't you?' came back the puzzled reply.

'Guess I'm feeling generous for a change. So it's your lucky day.'

At that moment Eleanor rushed across to comfort her father. 'You're a mighty tough jasper with that gun in your hand,' she rebuked the hired gunfighter.

Cole flipped the gun into the air and caught it by the barrel before offering it to her, butt first. 'You want to finish what your pa started, ma'am, then go right ahead.'

The girl ignored the gesture, being more concerned for her father. 'You all right, Dad?' she said, fussing over the bleeding injury.

'Guess I'll live,' came back the somewhat abashed reply. His hand hurt like the devil but it was only a flesh wound.

'Better get that hand fixed, mister, before you bleed to death.' With that parting piece of wisdom, Cole turned around and walked off, leaving Ed Clifford and his daughter rather mesmerized at this bewildering course events had taken.

'They say that guy is a ruthless adversary. That's why he's called the Kingpin.' Eleanor pondered, watching the tall stranger amble away as if he hadn't a care in the world. 'So why didn't he kill you?'

'That's what I been trying to figure out myself. It

don't make sense.' Ed Clifford was thinking back to another time, another place when the boot had been on the other foot.

The foreman had joined them and was all for making a far more terminal end to the confrontation. He drew his gun ready to finish off what he had started earlier that day. Clifford stayed his hand. 'No Dan! The fella has shown me some mercy. Reckon we should allow him the same consideration.'

Mather scowled. He was much less forgiving, especially when he perceived the hint of desire for his betrothed in the gunslinger's ardent gaze. But he held off, making a promise that his day of reckoning would come soon enough.

As Ed Clifford was being helped down the street for a visit to the sawbones, Cole entered the general store. Ivor Webb had been one of many bystanders fascinated by the recent showdown and its unusual conclusion. He was anxious not to upset the renowned gunfighter. A sycophantic manner greeted his latest customer. 'Anything I can get for you, Mr Jardine, just name it and it's your'n. No need to pay right now. Your credit is good with me.'

Cole hooked out the three empty cartridge cases. 'Do you stock these?' he said throwing them down onto the counter.

Webb inspected one of the brass cases closely. 'Errrrm!' he muttered to himself. 'I keep a few boxes of this type. Not much call for them round here, being they's from the Sharps Big Fifty buffalo rifle.' He looked up peering over his spectacles hoping to make a good impression. 'No buffalo around these parts. And there's only one guy I know of uses the Big Fifty.'

Cole waited. 'So are you going to enlighten me?'

'S-sure thing, Mr Jardine,' Webb blustered. 'It's Dan Mather, the guy who was all set to ventilate your hide out there if Clifford hadn't stopped him when you walked away.'

Cole raised his eyebrows. Two pieces of outlandish information, one of which was easy to fathom. But why would Clifford have stopped Mather finishing the job he had botched earlier that day? He was given no time to ponder on the enigma as the storeman continued.

'Him and Eleanor are hoping to get married. Dan will be taking over the Flying C when Clifford retires. Reckon he's done mighty well to have risen from a humble cowhand.' The store clerk threw Cole a knowing glance. 'Although my bet is that you and he have already met. That so?' Webb shrugged when no enlightenment was forthcoming. 'Anything else you want?'

'That's all I need to know for the present,' Cole said, heading for the door. There he hesitated, detouring over to the clothing shelves where he selected a pair of brown corduroy trousers and a grey flannel shirt. Returning to the counter he fished out a billfold.

Webb held up a hand. 'As I said before, sir. Your credit is good with me.'

'Much obliged. But I prefer to pay my way,' Cole

averred, handing over the requisite cost of his purchases. 'Cash on the barrel. I expect nothing less from my own clients.' A cool smile caused Ivor Webb to swallow nervously.

Back on the street a steely glint in Cole's eye boded ill for the previous owner of the three cartridges. He then headed back to his room at the National to enjoy a much needed bath. It would not even have entered his head had the delectable Miss Clifford not made the suggestion.

An hour later, freshly shaved and smelling a sight better than he had for some considerable time, Cole sauntered across to the Yellow Dog saloon. He had been reliably informed by the obsequious desk clerk that it was owned by Kez Randle. It was certainly a busy establishment, more upmarket than the usual down-at-heel bergs he visited. And it offered entertainment as well. A distinct bonus. On stage, a group of scantily clad dancers were hard at work supported by a lively quartet of musicians.

Their vociferous reception was nothing, however, to that delivered when the main act sashayed onto the stage. A melodious voice announced the appearance of a raunchy songbird who then proceeded to wow the audience with her rendition of a well-known favourite entitled 'The Boys from the Back Room'.

And that was yet another surprise for the hired pistolero.

Last time he had set eyes on the ravishing Lily Devine was in Denver when Waco had asked her to marry him. The guy was besotted. Lily had let him

40

down gently. Although that hadn't been any consolation to Cole's distraught partner. All three had drowned their sorrows in time-honoured fashion. When the two buddies had finally surfaced the next day, Lily had disappeared; left town on the first stage heading south, according to the agent.

That was the last time he had seen her. So it came as a huge surprise to find her working for the man who had sent the wire. Following her last song, Lily signalled for Cole to join her upstairs in the boss's private quarters.

'Been a long time, Cole,' Lily purred, handing him a glass of finest Scotch whisky. The mellifluous tone hardened as she added, 'Is Waco around?'

She quickly relaxed on hearing the answer. 'He's chasing sheep up in Medicine Bow country. But the poor guy is still holding that candle for you, Lily.'

The sultry singer sipped her drink while moving in closer. 'Waco's a nice enough guy. But you know there was only ever one fella for me, Cole.' A languid hand brushed against his chest. 'I know all about Kez's plan to take over the valley. That could be me and you if'n we play our cards right.' Puckered lips, soft and redolent, offered themselves up to the handsome gunslinger.

What might have happened was cut short when the door opened to admit Kez Randle. The two old acquaintances instantly moved apart.

'Glad to see you've finally decided to make an appearance, Jardine.' A smart jasper clad in the best attire money could buy as befitted his aspirations as a successful businessman, Randle's manner remained stiff and formal. He poured himself a drink. 'I see that Lily has already introduced herself.' A sour regard for his singer's assumed authority by occupying his own private domain was no less brittle as he continued, 'I don't like to be kept waiting. Especially by the man I've just hired.'

'Seems to me like you're taking an awful lot for granted, mister,' Cole retorted curtly. 'I haven't agreed to anything yet. And I don't like it when the whole town's expecting me, yet I'm the one left in the dark. If'n you wanted some jasper removed, you should have told me.'

'Some things are best said in person and not committed to paper.' Randle bit off the end of a Havana cigar and lit up. 'And you should have got rid of Ed Clifford when you had the chance. It would have saved me a lot of unnecessary hassle.'

'A bit late in the day for that,' Cole replied, helping himself to a cigar. Lily couldn't resist a sly smirk. 'So what's Clifford done that's so bad? Surely that old dude can't be causing a big shot like you so much trouble.'

'He owns some land that I want.'

'So why not just buy him off?'

'The stubborn critter won't sell.' For the first time, Randle's urbane image slipped back into the ruthless schemer lying beneath. His lip curled in anger. 'I've offered him more than the going rate. Luckily, the tornado that blew down from the north this spring wiped out most of the Flying C stock. It almost bankrupted him. To keep from going under he was forced to borrow money. And I was the only guy in Red Mesa willing to help him out. That dough is still owed. If he doesn't pay it back in a month, the ranch is forfeit. And I get what I want the easy way.'

Cole was still mystified. 'So what's the problem? A month ain't long to wait.'

'The problem, Mr Jardine, is that he's managed to secure a contract with the new army post at Fort Belvedere on the far side of the Spruce Mountains. I need you to ensure they never reach their destination.'

'And how am I expected to do that?'

'You're the hired gunslinger. I'm sure you'll figure out a way,' Randle snapped back. 'And I'm willing to pay you five hundred down, and another thousand when the job's done.' The sly operator stepped back, puffing on his cigar as if it were a done deal. 'So what do you say?'

A disparaging sneer greeted what Cole considered a derisory offer. 'I do all the hard work and you fill your pockets. I don't think so. A half share of the profits will be a fair return or I walk away.'

Randle was nonplussed by Cole's reaction. 'That's far too much. There are others who would snap my hand off for a deal like that.'

Cole stood his ground. 'So why send for me?' Cole answered his own question. 'Because you want the best. And that's gonna cost a sight more'n fifteen hundred bucks. Think it over, Mr Randle. I'll be downstairs in the bar when you're ready.' And with that snappy rejoinder, the Kingpin departed, leaving

43

the saloon boss fuming.

'You didn't exactly handle that with your customary aplomb, Kez,' Lily scoffed. 'So how you gonna bring him to heel?'

'I'll think on it overnight then make him a better offer. Every man has his price.' His black orbs narrowed to thin slits. 'One way or another, I aim to get that land. The railroad company is willing to pay big bucks to the guy that owns it. And that guy is gonna be Kez Randle.'

FIVE

SNAKE EYES WINS

As Cole wandered downstairs into the body of the saloon, he had much to think on. This was not turning out to be the kind of job he relished. Kez Randle was a shifty unpleasant dude who assumed far too much. And what was Lily's angle, getting mixed up with a shyster like that? She certainly appeared to be on more intimate terms with the guy than any normal entertainer. He shrugged. Perhaps she figured he would make an ideal sugar daddy. After all, none of them were getting any younger.

One thing was for sure. Randle would have to considerably up the ante to secure the services of the Kingpin. And even then, he felt uncomfortable going up against a guy like Ed Clifford who had done nothing to warrant his land being snatched away. It went against his sense of right and wrong.

These and other ramblings were swimming around

inside his head when a voice interrupted his cogita-
tions. He paused to see who had called his name. The
owner of the Flying C was seated at a green baize
table nearby, a bottle of whiskey close to hand. He
appeared to be quite relaxed, lounging in a saloon
owned by the guy who was after ruining him.

'Take a seat, Jardine. Let me buy you a drink.'
Cole's sceptical frown and stiff bearing produced a
degree of conciliation from the rancher. 'I ain't
gonna draw on you again if'n that's what you're
thinking. I've learned my lesson the hard way.' He
held up a bandaged hand.

The rancher's presence inside the enemy's den was
written large across Cole's surprised face. 'Ain't you
taking a big risk coming in here?' he enquired tentatively, sitting down.

Clifford shrugged off the suggestion. 'Randle
wouldn't try anything in his own place. Bad for business. I'm safer here than anywhere else in Red Mesa.
Ain't that so, Kez?'

The saloon owner had followed his recent visitor
downstairs. A defiant stare challenged Randle to
cause a ruckus in his own place. The speaker's arro-
gant sneer was matched by a scowl while the devious
critter took heed of what his adversary was planning.
It certainly was unusual for any of the Flying C crew
to frequent the Yellow Dog. Randle couldn't help sur-
mising what game he was playing.

Cole sat facing Clifford, who was casually playing
with a set of crap dice. A portly guy to his left was
introduced as Doc Chambers. It was the medic who

poured the drinks. The two principal participants clinked glasses. Yet only the rancher appeared to feel at ease.

On his other side lounged a good-looking fella in range garb who made no effort to welcome the new-comer. His manner was stiffly remote, distinctly on the chilly side. Could this be the mysterious bush-whacker? Cole's supposition proved to be right on the button when Dan Mather was introduced. The jigger's name drew an equally grim regard from the Kingpin. A hand reached for the empty cartridge cases in his pocket. But he held his peace, for the present.

'Guess you're wondering why I asked you to join me,' Clifford said, sipping his drink. He didn't wait for a reply. 'Fact is, you remind me of when I was a young tearaway back in the fifties. I ran with the Border Ruffians for a spell until Bill Hickok put me straight.'

'I never knew you ran with that bunch, Ed,' exclaimed the startled medic. 'You've sure kept that quiet all these years we've know each other.'

'Not the sort of information a guy wants bandying around, Doc. But without Wild Bill's guiding hand, I'd have been a permanent resident on Boot Hill years ago.' Clifford then turned his attention back to the man hired to kill him; the man who had gone against the grain of his kind and displayed a sense of clemency. 'My daughter tells me that you're hanker-ing after running your own spread, Mr Jardine.'

'I did mention something of the kind when we met on the stage,' Cole admitted, wondering where this

47

conversation was heading.

'You can have that chance right here and now. I'm willing to make that dream come true on a single throw of the dice.' The rancher rolled the pair of cubes across the table. 'Highest score wins. So what do you say?'

The gunfighter pondered over this unexpected turn of events. 'And what about the loan that's owing?' he asked.

A sly smirk was arrowed at the hovering saloon boss. 'That's the bit I'm more than ready to pass over. It's your call. You in or out? You'll never get a better chance than this.'

The proposal, bizarre in the extreme, was certainly worth considering. One thing was bugging him though. 'What happens if'n I lose?'

'You come and work for me. A hired gun on the payroll with the Kingpin's reputation will make it a sight easier to move those steer to Fort Belvedere.'

The rancher's startling attempt to stymie his underhanded scheme saw Randle butting in. 'Hold up there, Jardine. You're supposed to be working for me, not this old has-been.'

'I didn't agree to anything.' A frosty regard skewered the guy to the spot. 'Seems to me like you wouldn't have accepted my terms.' He returned his attention to Ed Clifford and his proposal. The winner-takes-all challenge had attracted a host of interested spectators. It wasn't every day that a ranch came up for grabs on the throw of a pair of dice.

Before a decision could be made Doc Chambers

issued a warning. 'You should know, Kingpin,' the medic's bulbously red snout jutted forward, 'this guy has never lost a craps game all the years I've known him.'

Cole smiled. 'Then it's about time his luck ran out. You have yourself a deal, Mr Clifford.' They shook hands on it.

'Glad to hear it,' the rancher espoused. 'And just to prove there's no cheating involved, we'll use a pair of house dice.' He held out a hand. 'If'n you please, Kez.' Unable to voice any objections, Randle complied. 'You first, Kingpin.'

Cole sucked in a deep breath and dropped the dice into the cup provided. He gave the black-spotted cubes a good shake before launching them across the green baize. All eyes followed the dancing dice as they cavorted like a pair of lively prairie dogs, finally coming to rest. A collective gasp issued from a myriad throats on seeing the result – a one and a three.

All the odds were now stacked in favour of Clifford retaining his spread and having the famous hired gunfighter working for him as a common ranch hand. Neither outcome offered any advantage to Kez Randle. The man he had hoped to hire would be on the opposing side in either case. The foiled schemer could only look on, his hands tied. Ed Clifford was not the simple cowpuncher he had figured.

It was now the wily rancher's turn. Clifford slowly gathered up the dice and followed a similar procedure but with a personalized ritual. Hand covering the open cup he shook them vigorously either side of his head while intoning a lucky rhyme. 'Shudder and shake the dice throw goes, how they fall nobody knows.' Then he slammed the cup down onto the table. Slowly the cover was lifted to expose . . . Snake Eyes!! He then quickly stuck the dice in his pocket.

The saloon erupted in exclamations of shocked surprise. None more so than Doc Chambers. 'Well I'll be a lop-eared mule,' he exclaimed, scratching at a thinning pate. 'I ain't never seen the like afore. Ed Clifford getting beat at craps.'

Clifford's own reaction was a restrained half smile of his own. 'Guess your supposition was right, Jardine. Looks like you've just won yourself a ranch.'

Randle was not about to give up that easily. 'Let me see those dice,' he snapped. The rancher dropped them on the table allowing Randle a closer examination. He tossed them onto the table a couple of times.

Clifford laughed out loud. 'Figured I was pulling a fast one by using loaded dice, Kez? You should know me better than that.' The saloon boss grimaced throwing them aside. So irate was he that the wily glimmer of subterfuge in the old rancher's narrowed regard passed unheeded. His next remark, surprisingly upbeat, was addressed to the mesmerized winner.

'Come out to the Flying C tomorrow, young fella, and we'll finalize the details.' Without uttering another word Clifford then stood up and left the saloon, followed by his foreman.

Cole remained in his seat for a spell trying to absorb the mind-blowing fact that he was now a ranch owner. All around him the babble of conversation focused on the startling result of the wager. He slung down a generous slug of whiskey then stood up slowly. 'I'll be moving a herd of cattle to market in a few days.' Although not ostensibly targeted, the blunt declaration was clearly aimed at the tight-lipped saloon owner. 'Anybody who tries to stop me will get more trouble than he can handle.' And with that parting comment he also departed.

Randle was seething. But there was little he could do to prevent Ed Clifford saving his ranch from going bankrupt. 'What you going to do now, Kez?' Lily asked, struggling to hide her own frustration. She had been deliberately wheedling her way into the sly jasper's affections with the intention of securing a slice of the action. That now appeared to have been thrown out with the bathwater.

'Nothing much I can do,' Randle grunted, arrows of hate stabbing the object of his wrath in the back. 'That guy is one mean *hombre*. None of my boys measure up to his reputation. I'll just have to cut my losses and look elsewhere.'

'Not necessarily,' Lily said, grabbing his attention.

'You got something in mind?'

'There's one guy who ain't scared of the Kingpin. But he won't come cheap. So if'n I do send for him, make sure this time you don't offer a cut-price deal.'

A fresh sparkle of expectation had been rekindled in Kez Randle's skeletal features. 'Who is this guy? And how long will it take him to get here? We ain't got much time now that Judas of a gunslinger has

51

swapped sides.'

'He's called Waco Santee and he's currently doing a clear-up job in Wyoming around Medicine Bow. If'n I send a wire, he should be here in six days.'

'Then what you waiting for, gal. Get to it pronto.'

Out on the street in front of the Yellow Dog, Ed Clifford was sitting astride his horse awaiting the arrival of his foreman who was buying some fresh Bull Durham and papers from the tobacconist's. Mather was rolling a querly and had just passed the front of the saloon when Cole emerged.

'Hold on there, mister,' the new ranch-owner called out. 'You forgot something.' When Mather swung on his boot heel, Cole threw down the empty cartridge cases. The blood drained from the foreman's face. The accuser's next remark was delivered in a menacing drawl, cold as a death wish. 'You should have finished the job when you had the chance. Now the odds have been evened out, let's see how you measure up.'

It was an icy challenge that could not be ignored. One that no bushwhacker ever wanted to face. But Mather had been given no choice if'n he wanted to retain any respect, a vital element of any frontiersman worth his salt. The whole town was watching as the two protagonists faced each other.

'It's your call, Mather. Now make your play or crawl back under the stone you came from.' Cole's blunt rejoinder triggered a thin coating of sweat to break across the foreman's brow. His fingers flexed in readiness for the inevitable draw.

Moments away from destiny's summons, Ed Clifford stepped between them. On first learning that his future son-in-law had taken it upon himself to ambush the hired gunman, bewilderment, disbelief even, had numbed the older man's brain. Jardine's demand for a one-to-one shoot-out stimulated an intervention.

'Don't do it, son.' The earnest appeal for clemency was aimed at Cole. 'Land sakes, you have every right to be angry. I'm darned sore as well. This fool had no business trying to take you out like that. But he was only trying to protect me.' He threw an angry glare at the other man. 'As you've already seen, Dan, I fight my own battles.' He held up the bandaged hand before turning back to address Cole. 'Just think on it before doing something you'll regret.'

Cole's face remained set, hard as a stone effigy. Bushwhackers were the lowest form of life. Especially a backshooter. Like a suppurating boil they needed lancing. Then his glance caught sight of a white face peering out of an upstairs window of the Drover's Cottage. A look of unqualified horror, of pleading to show mercy was written across the ashen features. If there was one person he did not want to antagonize further it was Eleanor Clifford. The exact opposite, if truth be told.

A smile was aimed at the pale face in the window. It immediately disappeared. But Cole was not concerned. Once he took possession of his newly won holding, there would time enough to make his presence felt.

His manner relaxed accordingly. 'Guess you've earned a reprieve, Dan. But one step out of line and there won't be no second chance.' He turned his back on the guy and walked away. 'See you in the morning, Mr Clifford. Bright and early.'

SIX

A BLUNT-EDGED RECEPTION

Cresting a ridge an hour's ride south of Red Mesa, the new owner of the Flying C land holding looked down upon the utopia of which he had long dreamed. It was the strange – if not bizarre – method of its acquisition that he found unsettling. Yet as his animated gaze panned across the rolling terrain, he could not help feeling a sense of jubilation; excitement that heralded a new beginning.

Ranch buildings that comprised a barn, stable, blacksmith's workshop and bunkhouse surrounded the two-storey main house on three sides. The whole caboodle was enclosed by a sturdy lodge-pole fence with a corral to one side where horses wandered at will. The entrance to the headquarters was dominated by a large letter C with eagle wings carved in wood on either side. An impressive sight to be sure. Cole pushed on down the slope, eager to acquaint himself with his new acquisition.

Passing beneath the striking entrance portal, he was met by the threatening presence of Dan Mather. The foreman was standing in the middle of the open sward in front of the house. Legs akimbo, bunched fists hanging by his side, this was no welcome meeting.

Mather was now on home ground, a fact that had strengthened his spirit of resistance. With the spread now in the hands of a hired gunslinger, the foreman knew that his chances of taking over the Flying C when Clifford retired had gone up in smoke. And he was mighty peeved to say the least. And being made to look a fool in Red Mesa with his girl looking on required a blunt response.

There was only one way to appease his frustration. Slowly and deliberately he unfastened his gunbelt and handed it to one of the other hands who were ranged up behind. Cole could see immediately where this was heading. But he was in no way fazed by the burly cowpuncher. The hired gun had been schooled in the noble art of prize fighting by a professional. His elder brother, no less. Rockpile Biff Jardine went on to become the northern territories bare-knuckle champion.

Cole had repaid the compliment by teaching his brother how to use a six shooter to maximum effect. They rode together for a spell up in Montana before Biff was killed during a botched robbery when a gang of desperadoes tried to rob the bank at Three Forks. The Jardine brothers had inadvertently arrived in the town in the thick of the action. The robbers had just emerged from the bank and all hell had broken loose. Hot lead flew every which way.

The violent confrontation with the vigilance committee led to a bystander being shot down as well as Biff Jardine. Neither survived. But nor did the three robbers whose bodies lay riddled with bullets outside the bank. Cole received a handsome reward for his part in thwarting the robbery. Wanted for murder and robbery across the territory, Ivory Jack Slocombe alone was worth a cool thousand.

But the money was no compensation for the death of a much-loved sibling. The mayor of Three Forks offered him the job of town marshal. Not wishing to be tied down to the place where his brother lay buried, Cole declined, instead heading down the trail of the hired gun.

That had been five years ago. He had teamed up with Waco Santee soon after. The well-matched duo's first job had been to protect gold shipments being transported from the Anaconda Mine down to the smelter at Billings. Various bad boys had tried to relieve them of their charge. None had succeeded. Their reputation had grown accordingly and numerous well-paid jobs followed.

Much water had flowed down the creek since then. And now Cole was the proud owner of a cattle ranch. All for the throw of a dice. He could still barely credit how Lady Luck had favoured him. But first he had to deal with this irksome glitch standing in his way.

It would not be plain sailing as the grim look of revenge being thrown his way by the aggrieved Dan Mather now testified. He stepped down and tied up his horse before addressing the waiting foreman. 'You sure this is what you want?' Cole cautioned the incensed ramrod who was snorting like an angry bull.

'Quit stalling, mister, and let's see how brave you are without them shooting irons to back your play.' Mather clenched his fists and moved forward intent on getting in the first punch.

The wild swing was easily deflected by his opponent, who moved in to deliver a solid right into Mather's stomach. The foreman doubled up, receiving a left hook to the chin. His teeth rattled inside his mouth, blood dribbling from a cut lip. Not a good start for the cocky puncher. His buddies quickly helped him up. Not wanting to admit defeat so soon into the contest, he shrugged them off, shaking the mush from inside his head.

Cole hunkered down into the prize-fighter's stance, fists raised one in front of the other. Mather wiped the blood from his mouth guffawing at what he judged to be a weak-kneed greenhorn posture. Real fighting men didn't prance about like showgirls. 'Look at this, you guys,' he sniggered to his pals. 'The clown figures he can dance his way out of this shindig.' But there were no supporting chortles from the watching hands. They had seen how the new owner had caught Mather flat-footed.

The smile slipped from the foreman's face as he

threw himself forward. Cole side-stepped and tripped the guy as he blundered past. Mather tumbled into the dust. Up on his feet in a moment, he again blundered forward displaying no subtlety of movement. It was no contest for a seasoned pugilist. A couple of solid jabs to the face brought the ham-fisted maladroit hardcase to a sudden halt.

But the foreman's method of brawling had been learned in saloons where no rules existed. Only the strongest or the most devious survived. And that is what the tricky foreman resorted to, knowing he could not beat this guy in a conventional fracas. He scooped up a handful of sand and tossed it into the face of his adversary. Cole staggered back, knuckles clawing at his eyes.

Mather was on him in a moment. Both men tumbled onto the ground, rolling about trying to gain the upper hand. This was where the foreman's brute strength gave him a distinct advantage. He forced Cole onto his back pinning him down with one hand, ready to deliver the lethal knockout blow. Cole knew that a rapid reaction was needed to save him from oblivion. Prize-fighting methods were of little use now. So he resorted to the mean-spirited tactics of his opponent. A hand reached up and gripped hold of the guy's privates, which he squeezed hard.

The result was instantaneous. 'Aaaaaaaaagh! Yuh lowdown skunk!' the victim yelled out, much to the hilarity of his watching pals. He rolled on the floor massaging the tender extremities. 'That ain't proper fighting. Them's dirty tactics.'

Cole stood over the cowed foreman. 'It takes one to know one, buster. You had enough yet?' But Mather was not beaten yet. His pride was at stake here. An arm cracked against the back of Cole's legs sending him tumbling to the ground. He jumped on top the fallen man. Once again they rolled across the ground, each struggling for the ascendancy.

On hearing the cacophony outside, Ed Clifford had come to see what all the commotion was about. Far from intervening, he leaned nonchalantly against a veranda post and watched. His daughter likewise had come outside. But she was far less tolerant of this animalistic behaviour. 'Why don't you stop them?' she remonstrated bitterly. 'Go on like this and one of them will be badly injured.'

'If'n that young fella intends to run this outfit, he needs to be tough. Going up against Dan will prove whether he has the guts to pull it off.'

'Well I'm not standing here like some ancient Roman baying for the blood of gladiators in the arena.' She grabbed a bucket which she dipped into the horse trough, tossing the contents over the grappling duo. The dousing certainly produced the desired outcome. Both men spluttered and gurgled as they rolled apart. 'On your feet you two. How dare you behave like wild dogs in my presence! You both ought to be ashamed of yourselves.'

'Guess we can call that a draw,' Clifford declared. 'What do you say, boys?' he asked the watching hands who nodded their agreement. 'Hey Jumble!' he

60

called across to the cook, who also doubled as the ranch medic for animals as well as humans. 'Get these two jackasses cleaned up.' Then to the new owner instructed, 'Soon as you're presentable, Kingpin, come into the house and I'll give you the paperwork to make this handover official.'

Without waiting for a reply, Clifford then went back inside. Having carefully observed how Cole Jardine had handled himself, he was well satisfied the guy had the makings of a solid rancher.

After struggling to his feet, the bedraggled and blood-smeared foreman tried desperately to appease his alleged betrothed. 'You ain't mad at me are you, honey?' he pleaded, trying to ingratiate himself back into the girl's favour. 'A guy has his pride. That prancing puppet needed taking down a peg to show him I ain't no milksop.'

'If'n you think that brawling in the dust like a common thug will impress me, Dan Mather, you're sadly mistaken.' No further words were spoken as the girl stamped off to join her father. Cole couldn't help pasting a sickly grin onto his face as she passed him. The girl immediately deflated his burgeoning ego with a cutting retort. 'And don't think you're any better in my estimation than him, Jardine. It's your arrival in Red Mesa that has caused all this trouble.'

'And I'm the one who's going make certain this place doesn't fall into the hands of Kez Randle,' was the new owner's crisp reply as he wiped a smear of blood from his knuckles. Eleanor ignored the poignant assertion, not wishing to bandy words with

61

this mysterious stranger who had so suddenly appeared in their lives.

'I hope you're satisfied.' Once inside the house, Eleanor proceeded to admonish her father. 'That hired gunslinger has only just turned up and already he's antagonized the whole crew.'

'I wouldn't be so sure of that,' Clifford countered. 'The fella certainly knows how to handle himself. Anybody who can match Dan toe-to-toe has certainly earned my respect. And I could see that the boys thought that as well. We need a solid guy like him to get the cattle to Fort Belvedere and keep Randle off'n our backs.'

The girl sniffed imperiously. 'I hope you're right, Dad. I surely do.'

'So do I, Elly,' her father intoned sombrely. 'If'n we don't meet that contract deadline by the end of the month, this place is finished. And Randle will have won.'

His daughter scoffed at the suggestion. 'That ain't your responsibility no more, Dad, seeing as how you've thrown it all away to that hired gunslinger. I don't know how you could have been so reckless to do such a thing.' Tears brimmed in her eyes. 'This place has been your whole life. I was born here.'

A hard cast framed the rancher's craggy face. 'I was desperate. And with that loan hanging over us, desperate measures were needed to stop the Flying C falling into the hands of that crooked panhandler. The Kingpin was hired to make sure the herd didn't reach Fort Belvedere. Now he has a vested interest to fulfil the contract.'

Eleanor peered suspiciously at her father as a hint of the truth emerged. 'Now I understand,' she averred firmly. 'You made sure Jardine would win that bet, didn't you? Some sleight of hand with those dice and low and behold, snake eyes!'

Clifford neither concurred nor denied the assertion. Then he smiled, the granite-moulded facade softening. 'Why don't you give the guy some slack, gal? We're gonna need him on our side.' Eleanor responded with a deep sigh as if to say she could never fathom the macho character inherent in all men.

At that moment Cole entered the office. 'How about that coffee then, Eleanor? Mr Jardine and I have business to conduct.' Then, as an afterthought, 'And don't forget to add some of them jam doughnuts you made this morning.' A poignant regard for discretion passed between father and daughter as Eleanor gave the newcomer a snooty flick of her lustrous hair before leaving the room.

'That daughter of your'n sure seems hard to please, Ed,' Cole declared.

'Don't worry, son,' the ex-rancher assured the new owner. 'She'll come round . . . eventually. Now let's get down to business.' He handed over the deed of ownership and the dreaded mortgage owed to Kez Randle. 'That's the bit I'm glad to get rid of.' They both signed the transfer document.

Once the official entrustment had been completed

with the traditional handshake, Clifford gave the new owner a cynical once-over. 'How much do you know about ranching, Cole?' he asked.

'I've done some punching up in Montana, but that ain't like running a spread the size of the Flying C,' Cole admitted.

'Then you're gonna need help.' The retired rancher paused. 'I can give you a quick rundown of the basics you'll need to know about organizing a drive. Then it's all your'n. But what about Dan? Can you work with him? He knows the business inside out and the hands respect him. Although judging by your performance outside, you should have no trouble on that score.'

'I ain't got no beef with Dan now. I can understand why he tried to dry-gulch me. Not that I approve. And I enjoyed proving that outside. Just so long as he knows who's bossing this outfit.'

Clifford nodded his agreement then lowered his voice, not wanting his daughter to earwig his next query. 'And what about Elly? I've seen how you look at her. And Dan has set his hat at marrying her.'

'I won't cause no trouble.' Cole kept a deadpan look on his face as he added, 'Just so long as he don't mind a bit of competition in that regard.'

The old timer concealed a sly smirk. He was rapidly arriving at the conclusion that he had made the right decision with this guy. As soon as they had finished the coffee and cakes, the two men went outside. Clifford had suggested they take a ride so that the new owner could see what he had acquired. They

64

were about to mount up when the hands arrived, led by Dan Mather.

'If'n you're still intent on rounding up the cattle and driving them to Fort Belvedere, the boys want paying what they're already owed,' the foreman said, directing his demand to Ed Clifford.

'We ain't received a darned nickel for two months, boss,' a wrangler by the name of Scooter Biggs piped up. 'Me and the boys signed up for thirty a month and found. All we've had so far is bed and board. We'd all like a trip into town to let off a bit of steam, instead of hanging around here every Saturday night.'

Clifford gave the claims an apathetic shrug, crossing his arms and leaning against the veranda. 'Ain't my problem no more, boys. Best ask the new boss.'

All eyes swivelled towards the hovering figure behind. This was a development that Cole had not foreseen. He looked questioningly at Clifford who provided the obvious response but not the solution. 'All the dough has gone on keeping this place going and these guys from going hungry. The safe is empty and so are my pockets. And its gonna stay that way until those cows are sold.' He stepped back gesturing for the somewhat bemused new owner to take the reins.

Cole took a deep breath before replying. He slowly stepped down off the veranda and faced the waiting hands. 'Seems to me that Ed's right. The only way for you guys to earn any dough is by getting those beasts to market. It's gonna be a tough job and there ain't a moment to spare if'n we're to meet the deadline.' He paused allowing the words to sink in. 'So I'm prepared to pay double the going rate when the job's completed. Until then, everybody, me included, works his ass off to make certain that happens.' He looked the men in the eye, silently urging them to concur with his stipulation.

Some much-needed support was provided by their old boss. 'I reckon that's a good deal, boys. Fact is, it's the only one on the table. Pull out now and you go away empty-handed. But stick around and you'll be in clover.' He kept quiet about the fact that Kez Randle was unlikely to let that happen without some form of brusque retaliation. Instead he maintained an upbeat mood of optimism. 'And I'm prepared to go along on the drive to add my backing to the new management.' He then turned to Cole. 'You can treat me like a regular hand with the same pay, not forgetting that bonus of course.' Smiles all round from the regular hands greeted this concession from their old boss.

What Clifford proposed was something Cole had not envisioned. His brow lifted in surprise. 'You're prepared to work for me after I took the ranch from you with the throw of a dice? I'm much obliged and sure would welcome your experience, Ed. But only if'n these guys are willing to go along.'

'So what d'you say, boys?' Clifford advocated confidently. 'Are we in this together, all for one and one for all?'

Biggs was the first man to voice his approval of the

deal. 'If'n you reckon we can do it, Mr Clifford, then I'm in.' One by one the others followed suit. It was left to Dan Mather to make his decision as the others wandered away.

'You willing to work under the new owner, Dan?' Clifford posited.

'Guess so, Ed. But I'm doing it for you . . . and Elly.' His loyalty was clearly not only to his old boss, but to the girl he still hoped to marry one day soon. And that could only happen if'n he stuck around and made sure that blamed gunslinger kept his hands to himself. A less than cordial regard passed between the two men as Mather rejoined his crew.

Cole was left under no illusions that this was going to be a difficult drive, and not only from the threat posed by Kez Randle. The tetchy foreman would not make life easy on the trail, that was for sure. But Cole was now the boss. And anybody who didn't pull their weight would be given short shrift.

Clifford appeared to read his thoughts. 'They're good hands, Cole, Don't go pushing them too hard. And you'll need Dan on your side,' he stressed. 'He's the only one familiar with the route to Fort Belvedere. It was Dan who secured the contract when we realized that driving them to the northern railhead was out of the question.'

No acknowledgement of the friendly advice was forthcoming as Cole stepped down off the veranda and mounted up. 'How's about you give me that personal viewing of what I've won? The sooner I get me a feel of the place, the sooner we can be on the trail.'

He tapped his pocket where the infamous mortgage paper was secreted. 'Every day wasted here is a benefit for Randle.'

SEVEN

ROUND UP

The two men rode silently for an hour with barely a spoken word between them. Each felt quietly at ease in the other's company. An early sun warmed their backs, its iridescent shimmer glancing off the distant upthrust of the Spruce Mountains. Flocks of meadow larks twittering and swooping with glee combined with deer cavorting at their leisure offered a scintillating sense of wellbeing. An idyllic tableau for a man yearning to cast off his gunfighting reputation and settle down.

The only bugbear, and no simple worry for any man, was the burning issue of saving the ranch from insolvency, the resolution of which was impossible to avoid. For the time being at least, Cole tried to distance himself from the problem he had inherited. Certainly there was no denying the beauteous nature of the Flying C holding. Yet even the dewy-eyed image of Eleanor Clifford could not prevent his mind harking back to the problem of Kez Randle.

Had he previously understood the true make-up of the situation he had blundered into, would he have accepted that challenge thrown down by his associate? Cole had never been one to brush aside difficulties encountered, instead facing them head on. And this was no different. No snake-in-the-grass like Randle was going to get the better of him. As such he harboured no regrets.

The ranch and the cultivated pastures were left behind as Ed Clifford led his companion further into the wild reaches of the realm he had so recently owned and managed. Rich grassland gave way to scrub vegetation in the rough foothills above the Gunnison valley. The further from civilization the duo progressed, however, the more furrows appeared on the young gunslinger's brow.

They had just arrived at the edge of a downfall overlooking broken country choked with dense thickets of mesquite and thorn bush. He drew to a halt, Ed Clifford by his side. 'There's a heap of rough terrain up this end of the holding,' the older man casually observed.

Cole made no comment. After much silent deliberation he posed the question that had been tumbling round inside his head for the last half hour. 'We've been riding for over two hours and I ain't seen a single cow,' the new owner remarked. 'You certain this is a cattle ranch? Cos I'm beginning to wonder.'

'We've only covered a quarter of the acreage so far. There's longhorns down there all right,' Clifford assured his young associate, 'but they were scattered to the four winds by the nasty twister that blew down the valley two months back. It only lasted for half a day. But that was enough to finish off the other ranchers. They were forced into selling out to Randle for a pittance.'

The explanation was cut short in mid-flow, a pensive yet gloomy expression conveying the anguish Mother Nature had caused. Cole looked away as the poor jasper wiped away a tear. The old rancher's grief was like the loss of a loved one. He knew better than to interrupt the morose cogitation.

Gathering himself together, Clifford breathed deep and carried on. 'We were lucky.' He pointed to a break in the far side of the valley. 'That box canyon over yonder saved us. If'n the storm funnelling down there hadn't blown itself out we wouldn't have been able to make this drive. As it was, half my stock were killed.'

'How long will it take to round them up?' Cole now realized the scale of the task he had been given.

'A week at least, providing we start straight away. Them critters will be strewn all over the place. It's a big job. Too much for an old guy like me to handle.' A shrewd look was fixed onto the younger man. 'Why do you think I let you have the spread? A hotshot hired gun of your calibre will make Randle think twice about causing more trouble. Last thing I want is that slimy tinhorn getting his hands on the land I've sweated blood over.'

Now it was Cole's turn to conclude that he had been fooled. 'So you deliberately threw that bet for me to win.' It was a blunt statement of fact.

'Having you in charge will make life much harder for that critter.' Clifford chuckled at the notion. 'It sure upset Mr Big Shot Randle's plans for an easy conquest, that's for sure. Now it's up to you, son. I've placed all my hopes in you. Don't let me down. Once the herd has been delivered to market, you can pay me off along with the rest of the boys and I'll retire peacefully.' Then he nudged his horse down the slope. Cole followed, struggling to get his head round the way fate had played its devious hand.

Around four in the afternoon, they were back at the ranch. Cole called all the hands together and apprised them of the work to be done. Ed Clifford stood to one side not deigning to interrupt. Dan Mather was the first to confirm his old boss's assertion that it would take a week to gather up all the strays into a single bunch.

Cole nodded slowly as if considering the difficult task ahead. 'Guess that's with working regular hours, ain't it?' Nobody disagreed. 'Well these are irregular times, men. And I want the drive ready to start first thing on Monday morning.'

The foreman was none too pleased when Cole made his demands known. He scoffed at the greenhorn rancher's inexperience. 'You crazy!' he exclaimed hotly. 'That's only three days off. I know this land inside out, a sight better than you. So I'm telling you, mister, it can't be done in that time. Ask the man who knows if'n you don't believe me.' He looked to Ed Clifford for support.

The old rancher merely shrugged his shoulders. 'Ain't my call, Dan. If the new owner wants it done, then I say get to it and stop carping.'

Cole took a step nearer to the foreman, a move intended to assert his authority. The critter who had tried and failed to dry-gulch him needed to know his place. Sharp eyes drilled into the simmering foreman though his orders were intended for them all. 'We'll work flat out until those steers are rounded up, night and day if'n needs be. You want some rest? Then sleep in the saddle. I'm sure you've all done it before. And I'll be there right alongside of you. Let nobody say that Cole Jardine is an office-bound johnny.'

'You heard the man,' Clifford endorsed his young protégé. 'And don't think because I've retired this ain't no concern of mine. I'm coming along like I always did in the past.' He smiled, adding a lighter touch to the tense atmosphere. 'Just to make sure nobody falls off'n his horse.'

The hands laughed along with him. 'Guess if'n you're ready and willing, Mr Clifford, we'll sure do our bit as well,' commented a hand known as Whiskey Joe.

'And that extra bonus will sure help keep me awake,' added Biggs.

'What about you, Dan?' ask Clifford. 'You in or out?'

'Seeing as you've given your blessing to this madcap shebang,' the foreman conceded with some reluctance, 'I'll pull my weight along with the others. But don't blame me if'n it all goes wrong.'

'That's settled then,' Cole said, thankful for Clifford's backing. 'Get yourselves some grub and an early night. You're gonna need it.' Once the men had departed, he expressed his reservations about the surly foreman.

'He's going along mainly to keep an eye on Eleanor,' Clifford remarked. 'She likes to help out with the cooking. Guess he don't trust her being alone with a handsome dude like you along.'

Cole poured scorn on the notion. 'Alone? I should be so lucky,' he grumbled with a desultory shrug. 'With the whole crew around to cramp my style, there ain't much hope of any progress in that direction.'

'That's not the way he sees it.'

The man in question was unsaddling his horse, but kept arrowing barbed looks at his rival. Cole was in no way fazed by the guy's antagonism but knew that sometime soon there would have to be a reckoning.

Clifford was well aware of that notion and quickly drew Cole's attention to another hand waiting nearby. 'You've already met the most important guy on any drive. And Jumble here can turn out a feast fit for a king in the middle of a storm.'

Cole threw a sceptical eye towards the portly jasper wearing a grubby apron and holding a large ladle. He sure didn't exude the regal reputation ascribed to him. 'Strange kinda name?' he said, shaking the free hand that was caked in sourdough mixture.

'My real name ain't for bandying around so I stick to Jumble,' the cook declared. 'It came about due to my son-of-a-gun stew. Everything gets thrown into the pot. Best you ever tasted, I guarantee.'

'And I wholeheartedly endorse that,' interjected Clifford. 'So what can we do for you, Jumble?'

'We're running short on supplies, boss.' It would take some time to accept the new recipient of the title. 'Only around five days left. And I heard a whisper that the money has run out. I was just wondering what I'm meant to serve up when the real drive starts.'

'Write me out a list of everything you need,' Cole assured the rotund stomach filler. 'I'll make sure you get it.' That seemed to satisfy Jumble who wandered back to the cookhouse. He had no idea how the supplies would be replenished, nor did he care. That was the boss's responsibility.

The following morning, Jumble had roused the hands before daybreak as instructed. Bacon and beans with hot biscuits washed down by mugs of strong Arbuckles set them up for the day. A half-hour later they were all in the saddle. Mather had divided the hands into three groups. Each was assigned to scour every nook and cranny, driving the scattered cattle to a central holding point where a natural basin allowed easy bunching. Cole and Ed moved between the groups while Jumble and Eleanor trundled along the valley bottom in the chuck wagon.

A break at noon for chow was interrupted by Cole arriving late to find Mather chinwagging with his alleged fiancée. She appeared to be showing undue concern for his bruised features following the recent set-to. Their closeness, smiling and canoodling, was like a red rag to a bull for the dust-caked rider. 'You got nothing better to do, Dan?' he snapped out. 'There's still plenty steers out there.'

'We're allowed a chow break, ain't we?' retorted the grumpy foreman. 'Me and the boys have been working non stop all morning.'

'And you'll carry on until all these beeves are corralled. Now shift your ass pronto!' The two adversaries faced off.

But it was Mather who backed down. 'OK boys, you heard the *bossman*,' he grudgingly ordered, laying a sarcastic bite onto the irksome status. 'Back to work.'

Cole grabbed himself a mug of coffee and a plate of refried beans, polished off in double-quick time and was back in the saddle when Eleanor pulled him up short. 'Do you have to be so hard on Dan?' she railed. 'He's gotten the best interests of the Flying C at heart.'

A mocking guffaw greeted the curt belief. 'More like he wants to make sure I don't butt in on his territory.' His eyes wandered over the girl's willowy figure. 'Can't say that I blame him.'

The girl's face reddened, a hand swung back ready to deliver a resounding slap to the grinning maw above. Cole saw it coming a mile off and grabbed the flailing arm. 'No need to be so touchy, ma'am,' he mocked lightly. 'That no-account rannie will never be the right guy for you.'

'Meaning you will?' came back the snappy rejoinder without waiting for a reply. 'In your dreams, mister.'

But Cole was not to be put off. 'You certainly are, Miss Clifford. No doubt about it.' The witty riposte saw him swinging away. A bright smile and a doffed hat left the girl speechless and alone, save for Jumble who had been listening in. He shook his head. What these young folks got up to in their spare time left him bemused. Best to keep his own counsel on that subject and get on with concocting a rabbit and potato pie for supper.

The round-up which continued apace over the next couple of days was no ordinary gathering in of cattle in which other ranchers participated and the branding of new stock took place. It was far more complex, involving the search for Flying C stock that had been driven every which way by the rogue tornado.

All cowboys looked forward to the regular spring round-ups when they met up with pals working on neighbouring ranches. In addition to the hard work of sorting cattle and the branding, much fun was enjoyed after the day's work was over. Musical instruments would be brought out with a good old sing-along round the campfire. Mock trials were often held with those found guilty made to ride a wild young steer.

77

Nothing like that on this round-up. It was a pure and simple matter of survival, and as such was no laughing matter for all those involved. Succeed and there would be extra dough in their pockets. But fail and they would all be out of work and back on the drift. Something no puncher wanted mid-season when all the best jobs had been allocated.

The serious nature of the current round-up came to a head that night when Dan Mather caught one of the other hands, a guy called Lincoln Doby, peeking through some bushes where Eleanor was stripped down and washing in a creek. A fight broke out and serious injury was only averted by Cole Jardine's intervention.

'There'll be no scrapping during this drive,' he iterated, firmly dragging the combatants apart. 'You have a beef with someone, leave it until after you've been paid off.'

'I ain't standing for any sonofabitch eyeballing my gal,' Mather snarled, attempting to resume the fracas. Cole's fist shot out. The solid blow connected with the foreman's jaw, knocking him sideways.

'You heard what I said. Any more of this and you're fired.' His own eyes strayed to the girl who was continuing with her ablutions totally oblivious of the upset her actions had caused. 'Can't say as I blame you one bit, Doby,' he added with a wry grin. Then to the foreman, 'You don't want the boys getting an eyeful, then send her back to the ranch. It's your call. But no more squabbling while I'm in charge.'

The two adversaries squared off, eye to eye. Cole didn't want another scrap. But no way could he display any sign of weakness in front of the other men. So he deliberately prodded the foreman in the chest. 'Make your mind up, Dan. Do as you're told or pull out.'

On any cattle outfit the ranch owner was king of all he surveyed. Only the bravest or most foolhardy bucked his undisputed authority. Dan Mather was neither, just a regular cowpuncher who was good at his job. But just to ensure the hands maintained their respect for his status he called out brusquely, 'I need a fresh horse from the remuda, Scooter. Go get it. And Idaho, take two men over to those breaks on the west quarter. I spotted some strays in there.'

Cole heaved another sigh of relief. Another hurdle surmounted. How many more would there be? Only time would tell.

Around the same time as the round-up was taking place, Waco Santee found himself drawing up outside the Yellow Dog saloon. He was intrigued by the wire sent by Lily Devine, particularly when it hailed from the town to which his old partner had been headed. Luckily the job for which he had been hired in Wyoming had just been satisfactorily concluded. The sheepherders had been left with no misunderstandings as to their fate should they venture onto cattle-only land in the future.

Lily had just finished her afternoon spot when Waco shouldered through the batwing doors. No bright smile of welcome greeted her old flame. A curt shake of those russet locks was enough to see him following her up the stairs where Kez Randle was mulling over how best to prevent the new owner of the Flying C from reaching Fort Belvedere. The latest news delivered by his spies was that the cattle had been rounded up and were ready for the main drive.

Randle wasted little time in small talk. 'We have a big problem, Mr Santee,' he declared, pouring them both a glass of Scotch. 'Lily tells me you are the best man to block the cattle ranching ambitions of Kingpin Jardine.' The saloon boss studied the newcomer closely before continuing, 'He's become something of a burr under my saddle that needs removing, and quickly. You ready to go up against your old partner?'

Waco was equally reticent in his manner. 'As I understand it, Cole came here to work for you, Mr Randle. And now you're telling me he's gone over to the opposition. Maybe you should fill me in before I make a decision.' Before Randle could speak, he turned to Lily. 'And what's your angle in all this? It's been a long time since you upped sticks and disappeared from Denver. Then suddenly, out of the blue, I get a message to get down here pronto.'

'Lily and I have got, shall we say, certain plans, Mr Santee,' the suave businessman interjected. 'That's all you need to know for the moment. As for Jardine. . . .' He then went on to explain succinctly what had happened that required Santee's special kind of contribution.

Having listened to the bizarre train of events, Waco

paced the room drawing hard on a cigar as he digested the import of what had been related. 'That's some story,' he said. 'But working on the other side of the fence from an old buddy ain't something I take lightly. It's gonna cost you, mister.'

'So what figure are we talking about?' asked the sceptical villain.

Waco had already decided what such action was worth. 'A thousand down and four more when the job's done. And it's not up for discussion. Take it or leave it.'

Randle was about to protest when Lily butted in. 'He'll agree to your price, Waco. Just make certain you deliver the goods.'

Teeth gritted, Kez Randle struggled to maintain an outwardly calm persona. The scheming rogue might have plighted his troth to the sultry singer, but that didn't give her carte blanche to make decisions on his behalf. 'I agree to your terms, Mr Santee. But as Lily says, I expect results that will give me overall control of the Flying C land.'

The gunman nodded, then threw a disparaging look at the woman he had once coveted. 'You've changed, Lily. And not for the better. Me, I'm just a gun for hire. But I never figured you'd be so eager to dry-gulch an old friend.'

'A gal has to look to her future, Waco. And singing for drunken cowpokes twice a day is not my idea of heaven. Kez here has offered me a way out.' The declaration was blunt and to the point, the implication clear as the driven snow. Without uttering another word she left the room.

'Now that we've sorted out the irksome business of payment for your services,' Randle declared, reluctantly handing over the initial remuneration, 'perhaps you could start earning that dough by suggesting how we can wreck Jardine's plans.'

EIGHT

STAMPEDE!

The cowboy's worst fear on a drive was a stampede. They were especially likely to erupt at night after the cattle had bedded down. Sudden and violent, there was often no warning as the whole herd scrambled to its feet. Anything or nothing could spook a herd. A clap of thunder, flash of lightning, jingle of spurs, a cracking twig, the list was endless. Two-year-old heifers were reckoned to be the most nervous.

Suddenly the whole caboodle would be on the move, charging like a single entity with no aim or purpose. The ground shook beneath pounding hoofs. To those caught up in the maelstrom it felt like they were in the centre of an earthquake. A terrifying experience for the uninitiated, it was hell on the hoof. Response had to be immediate if a catastrophe was to be averted.

The only way to prevent a herd from scattering in

all directions was for the cowboys to turn the rampaging beasts into a circle where they could mill themselves to an exhausted standstill. Not always possible if the terrain was broken up. It was common for animals to be scattered over a wide area, taking days to recover. Worse still was the loss of flesh, which could only be replaced by good grass.

The stampede that hit the Flying C herd during the night before the drive proper was no accident. Half a dozen gunshots were all that was needed to frighten the cattle and set them on the prod. Waco Santee had positioned his men on both sides of the grazing herd. In the flick of a gnat's wing the previous hard work had been effectively destroyed. Already tired out after following the tough round-up, the cowpokes were in no shape to pursue a thousand head of cattle running amok.

The aggressors had been given strict orders that none of the nighthawks guarding the herd were to be killed. Once their grim task had been successfully accomplished, they disappeared into the night. But in effecting a stampede, there is always the risk of things going awry. Scooter Biggs had found himself in the centre of the rampaging herd. His horse was bungled to the ground, its rider trampled under a myriad of stamping hoofs.

Only when daylight announced its presence was Cole able to ascertain the grim truth. The remains of the dead wrangler were barely recognizable. His close pal Idaho Blue carried the body across to flat ground where a makeshift grave was dug. Here

Biggs was laid to rest by the side of the trail. A wooden cross marking the spot was surrounded by grim-faced hands as Ed Clifford led the brief eulogy. Later, back in camp, Cole was eager to learn the hard facts concerning the aftermath of the heinous attack. 'What do you reckon?' he asked Dan Mather who had been scouring the valley with the rest of the crew.

'They're scattered all over the darned valley,' the foreman declared in a forthright manner. 'It'll take a week to gather them in. Whoever spooked the herd knew exactly what they were doing.'

'And I don't need to guess who was at back of it,' Cole snarled.

'You figure Kez Randle would be able to organize something like that?' Clifford said, expressing his doubt with a curl of the lip. 'Don't seem likely to me. He's a gambler. And his boys sure ain't cattle men.'

'He must have had help then,' Cole persisted. 'You know anyone else around here who would do this?' Clifford had no answer to that proposition. 'No way is that skunk gonna wreck this drive.' Cole gritted his teeth. 'I want those steers rounded up and ready to move day after tomorrow.'

'It can't be done,' Mather protested. 'The boys are done in already.'

'I don't want to hear excuses,' was Cole's blunt reaction. 'You can't do it, then clear out and I'll do the job myself.' Fists clenched he was ready to dish out more of his previous violent response to the recalcitrant foreman. Cole was good and mad, and not about to swallow any dissention from this two-bit agitator.

'Not on your own you won't,' asserted Clifford, quickly butting in to avert any discord. 'I'll die in the saddle before I let Randle get his dirty hands on this land.' He stepped forward addressing the perturbed foreman. 'We've known each other a long while, Dan. I never took you for a quitter. We're all in this together, sink or swim. And I need you to get this drive completed. If nothing else, do it for Scooter.'

Mather's faced reddened under the praise from his old boss. 'OK, Ed. Guess you're right. Me and the boys will do our darndest to make this work.' A less than cordial follow-up was aimed at the tense interloper. 'Scooter's dead so I'll be doing it for you and Eleanor.'

'That's good enough for me, Dan.'

'Enough of this jawing,' Cole butted in. 'Let's get back to work.'

As the edgy standoff broke up, Jumble the cook was hovering at Cole's elbow. 'Some'n I can do for you?' he snapped.

'You might not have noticed it, boss,' the cook began somewhat tentatively, 'but over the last couple of days the stew has contained some rather . . . erm,' Jumble paused to find the right word, '. . . shall we say unusual items.' Cole frowned wondering what his stomach had been digesting. The cook hurried on. 'And being an inventive sort of guy, I've done my best to keep everybody well fed. But now we're plumb out of regular grub and that includes the basics as well.'

He handed a note to the boss. 'Here's the list you asked for before the round-up started.'

Cole studied the list thoughtfully. He turned to Clifford. 'I'm assuming our credit is still accepted in Red Mesa?' he asked.

'Far as I know, Ivor Webb hasn't blacklisted us yet.'

'Head for town straight away, Jumble,' Cole ordered the cook. 'Sign any credit note you're given in my name. And while you're there, add three boxes of .45 revolver shells and one of Winchesters to the list. I'm down to what's left in my shell belt.' Old habits that had saved his life on more than one occasion died hard.

Over the course of the day, slowly but surely the scattered herd was rounded up. There would be no let-up for the hands if the time limit set by the new boss was to be met. They had all come to realize that Cole Jardine was a hard taskmaster, but one who displayed no favouritism. Their respect for the guy had matured on seeing him prepared to knuckle down to the hard graft just like a regular hand.

Only Dan Mather continued to harbour any resentment, although he made sure to keep it under wraps, for the time being. The green-eyed monster of jealousy continued to eat away at his vitals. Sooner or later the festering sore eating away inside would burst asunder.

Just when things appeared to be picking up, another problem arrived back in the form of the disgruntled cook. 'That slimy rat of a storekeeper turned me away,' Jumble complained. 'Reckons our credit ain't worth a plugged nickel no more.'

Cole growled into his coffee mug. 'Well I ain't standing for that.' He called across to Eleanor who was washing the dishes. 'On your feet, girl, we're going into town.'

The girl balked at being ordered around. 'Why can't Jumble go? He knows the grub situation better than me.'

'No offence, Jumble,' Cole replied with a smirk. 'But you ain't exactly what I need for this delicate task.' He turned back, softening his voice to entice Eleanor. 'I need you to work your feminine wiles on the critter. Maybe fluttering your eyelashes will soften him up. If that don't work, then I'll have to use more forceful means.'

Eleanor was none too pleased at being used in that manner. 'I didn't come on this drive to act as your mediator.'

'You came on this drive to obey orders.' Cole's reply was flat but with a distinct hint of disdain. 'We'll be leaving in five minutes.' When they arrived in Red Mesa, Cole had substantially moderated his standpoint. He had no wish to antagonize this lovely creature, in fact the exact opposite. But he had to maintain an air of detachment in front of the crew. 'I need to go and have this out with Randle,' he said drawing the wagon to a halt behind the general store. 'And I need to do it alone. Meet me round the front in fifteen minutes.'

Eleanor's demeanour had likewise softened towards this enigmatic stranger. 'You will be careful, won't you? That guy is slippery as a wet fish.'

Cole's face lit up. 'So you don't think I'm such a bad guy after all? And what about Dan? Where does he fit into the picture? The guy seems to think you're going to become Mrs Mather.'

'Dan can think what likes,' she snapped back. 'I make up my own mind.' The strong-willed, decisive character had reasserted itself. 'My main concern at the moment is making sure we get those cattle to market and save the ranch. Even if it will be owned by an outsider.'

Five minutes later, Cole pushed his way into Kez Randle's private office. 'I've come to issue a warning, Randle. Keep away from my cattle. I know it was you that spooked 'em the other night. A couple of days and we'll be on the trail. Try any more funny business and I'll come looking for you with this.' He flourished the nickel-plated Colt Peacemaker in the gambler's face.

The sudden intervention of his nemesis stonewalled the gambler. 'I don't know what you're talking about,' he blustered, before quickly recovering his composure. 'How dare you bust in on a private discussion.'

Cole ignored the posturing villain. 'I know it was you who stampeded those cattle.' An accusatory finger underscored the rat's culpability. 'But you ain't gonna win. Neither are you gonna stop me getting the supplies I need.'

'You can't threaten me, Jardine,' came back the measured reply. 'I'm not acting alone anymore. I've

89

brought in help that's going to block any move you make.'

'You talking about those clowns downstairs? Don't make me laugh.'

'Never figured I'd be seeing you again this soon, Kingpin.' The sudden interjection came from a side room from which a familiar figure now emerged. 'But in our game, a guy has to take any work he can get. Providing of course it pays good.'

'Waco! What in thunder are you doing here?' Cole was genuinely taken aback by the appearance of his old partner.

'No secret there, old buddy. I'm working for Randle. He's prepared to pay big bucks to get you out of his hair.' Waco smiled knowingly, although his partner couldn't help but pick up on the hard-edged quip that followed. 'A guy wants the best, he pays for it.'

Still, Cole couldn't help chuckling. 'Exactly what I told this varmint. Ain't that so, Mr Randle?' He wagged a finger under the guy's nose. 'But the tight wad tried short-changing me. That was a bad move as you've discovered.' Randle spluttered, helplessly lost for words. Cole offered the dude a mocking curl of the lip. 'So, Waco, how's about we talk this dilemma through over a drink?'

'Sure thing, buddy. I'm all for that,' his pal grinned as he took Cole by the arm and led him out the room, leaving Randle fuming but impotent to do anything. Lily was in the middle of a song-and-dance routine so they just took a seat and watched the floor show. 'She sure is one special dame. A darned waste, her teaming up with a guy like Randle,' Santee adjudged, sipping his drink. 'Maybe when this job is finished, I can persuade her to swap sides.'

'You're assuming a mite too much there, ain't you pal?' Cole said. 'My job is to get that herd to market.' He paused, holding the other man's challenging exigent gaze. 'And I ain't gonna let anyone stop me.' The threat to any interference with his objective was palpable. Suddenly the inevitable tension that had been simmering ever since the two old pards had met threatened to boil over. It was only the ending of Lily's spot and her joining them that prevented any rash action from blowing up. 'Just like old times,' she commented, sitting between the two men. 'Last occasion if'n I recall was in the Denver Queen.'

'Not quite the same though,' Cole remarked, eyeing his old pard over the rim of his glass. 'This time we're on opposite sides of the fence.' He was about to add a further upshot when he noticed Eleanor by the door. 'Better think hard about who you're taking on here, Waco. But for the moment I have other business that needs my undivided attention.'

Lily scowled at the pretty girl. 'Figured a guy like you would have set his hat at somebody more classy than a ranch gal.'

'You learn something new every day, Lily,' he remarked casually. And with that snappy comeback he joined Eleanor outside. 'Any luck with Webb?'

91

A downcast shake of the head told its own story. 'The guy won't budge. He says we owe too much already and until it's paid, there's no more credit.'

Cole's mouth tightened with anger. 'This is all Randle's doing. He must have threatened the guy. We're gonna get those supplies. I'll make sure of that.'

'I don't want you inflicting any violence on him.' Eleanor's stipulation was adamant. 'I'd rather live off saddle leather and gopher meat if'n he won't play ball.'

Cole offered her a watery assurance he had no intention of keeping. 'You drive the wagon round back of the store so we can load up in private. I'll let you know when I'm ready.'

Cole found Ivor Webb doing his yearly stock check. 'I've come to take up your offer of credit,' he declared light-heartedly. 'Here's the list. You'll be paid once my herd has been sold to the army at Fort Belvedere.'

The storekeeper refused to be co-operative. 'As I told Miss Clifford, it's cash on the barrel. I can't give any more credit to that family.'

'You're giving it to me, Kingpin Jardine, the rough, tough hired gunslinger who don't take no for an answer.' Cole fixed his most malevolent look on the scared guy. 'Now, you gonna oblige or do I shove this list where the sun don't shine and get the goods myself? One way or another I ain't leaving here without them.'

'I-I'd sure love to h-help you, Mr Jardine, but I just

can't.' Cole felt sorry for the poor jasper. He was terrified out of his wits.

'Randle been putting on the squeeze?' The imploring look told him all he needed to know. 'Well you can tell him the truth. I came in here threatening to shoot you. Now get those supplies marked off. I ain't gotten time to argue anymore.'

While this altercation was being played out, Lily was questioning Waco about his intentions regarding their mutual associate. 'Think you'll have to kill him?' she hesitantly enquired.

That was an unsavoury trail down which the hired gunman was loath to travel. He stared morosely into his drink, swirling the amber contents to focus his thoughts. 'Cole isn't about to give up without a fight. You know that as well as I do. He'll fight tooth and nail to get what he wants. He ain't the Kingpin for nothing.'

'So what you gonna do?' Lily pressed him. 'Kez wants that land and he's paying you well to ensure he gets it.'

'Don't tell me what I already know, Lily,' Waco retorted waspishly. 'Now give me some space to think.' The singer knew when to hold her tongue as she watched her old flame's furrowed brow puzzling over his next move. She stood up and moved away, wondering if she had done the right thing in bringing these two old buddies into conflict.

Waco's back stiffened. He recalled that Cole had come to Red Mesa as much for fresh supplies as his beef against Randle. And he adjudged correctly that the Kingpin would have headed for the general store to take what was required. He was on his feet in a moment. He signalled to five men standing idly at the bar. 'Over here, you guys. We have work to do.'

None of the men dissented. Randle had given strict instructions that Waco Santee was now in charge of any nefarious tactics to undermine the Flying C cattle drive. It was Santee who had organized the stampede. And he now intended to prevent his pal completing the drive by the deadline, hopefully without any blood being spilled. But should any resistance be encountered, Santee would not be deterred from completing his task by any past bond of loyal affiliation.

Quickly and concisely, he explained his plan to the assembled hard cases.

NINE

CAPTURED . . .

The supplies had already been collected and stored in the wagon out back when Santee and his subordinates gathered outside the store. Inside, totally oblivious of the imminent threat to his wellbeing, Cole was studying the list to ensure everything had been included. Satisfied, he then appended his signature. 'Don't worry about being paid,' he appeased the disgruntled clerk. 'You'll get your money soon as I've sold those cattle.'

'Randle is gonna be mad as hell when he finds out,' Webb grumbled.

'Just tell him that Cole Jardine gave you no choice in the matter.' A mirthless smile crossed the gunslinger's face. 'He'll understand.'

His back was to the door through which Waco Santee was now peering. The gunman's face creased in a grim smile. He and his men had arrived at just the right moment. Santee cast a wary look up and down the street to ensure no prying eyes were witness to what was about to take place inside the store.

'No guns!' was his blunt order to the Randle heavies. 'We don't want the whole town knowing our business.' A piercing gimlet eye left the toughs in no doubt who was in charge. 'We give him the chance to come quietly. Only if'n he cuts up rough do we use force. Savvy?' Curt nods registered their accord.

Following that stipulation, they burst through the door. Cole was caught unawares, left flat-footed, by the sudden intervention of the invaders led by his old partner. 'Don't make this difficult for yourself, Cole,' the gunman rapped out, brandishing his pistol. 'I'll use this if'n I have to. Randle just wants you out the way until the deadline runs out.'

Although startled by the sudden intervention, Cole retained a cool head. 'You didn't waste much time, did you?'

The measured remark received no answer as the two men faced each other. Silent and unmoving, each held the ice-coated stare of the other for no more than a half-dozen eye blinks. But Cole was loath to surrender without a fight. It was not in his nature, and Santee recognized the stubborn streak in his tightly clenched fists.

Ivor Webb also saw the signs and shrunk back, anxious to avoid getting caught up in the exchange he knew was coming. Yet still Santee issued a salutary warning hopeful of averting a lethal fracas.

'Don't do it, Cole,' he warned his buddy. 'You

won't stand a chance. Even the great Kingpin can't beat the six of us. Surrender now and I'll go easy on you.' In his heart he knew that Cole would never give in. So he made sure that his adversary was neutralized. 'Lift that gun out the holster nice and slowly and slide it over here.' His own weapon, held steady as a rock, gave Cole little choice but to comply.

'I somehow knew that one day we'd be forced to go up against each other,' Cole replied playing for time. 'Guys in our line of work can never hope to remain on the same side for ever.'

'You're right there, pal,' Santee agreed. 'Guess now we'll never find out which of us is the fastest draw.'

The ruffians lined up behind Santee were growing edgy. All this chinwag was getting to their nerves. 'Enough of this jawboning,' rasped one tough called Poke Adderly. 'Let's do what we came for.'

Santee ignored the tough's gripe, waiting for his old pard to make the first move. The world stood still in Webb's General Store. But only for a long second or two as the clock on the wall ominously ticked away. It was the jarring chime on the quarter hour that precipitated Cole into action.

He grabbed a wooden pitchfork handle and swung it, connecting with Waco's hand. Caught out by the surprise move, a cry of pain issued from the guy's open mouth as he released the gun, which clattered to the floor. Head down Cole charged at the tight gathering, scattering them like skittles. The dim light cast by a single tallow lamp assisted his frantic attempt to escape. If he could only reach the door, he stood a chance. But, as predicted, six against one were poor odds for success.

One foe at the edge of the group stuck his boot out, pitching the fugitive headlong onto the floor. The others were on him in a moment. Desperation and the will to survive, however, are apt to spur a man to untold feats of retaliation when the chips are down. Cole was no exception.

Battling like a man possessed he swung hard fists left and right. Bone struck bone. Pained grunts and angry growls testified to the cornered man's resolve to remain at liberty. Shadows like dancing marionettes flashed across the wooden walls as the uneven struggle flickered back and forth. Haunting shapes gave the impression that a devilish picture show was in progress. Yet this was no chimera, no figment of a demented imagination. The blows thudding against bodies were real enough, the gasps of punishment received indisputable.

Cole fought on grimly. And he might have succeeded had the odds been less stacked against him. Alas, it was not to be. There were indeed too many for one man to overcome. And it was his old pal who brought the unequal fracas to an abrupt finale. Santee's hand was aching from the original blow. Luckily it was not broken. Nonetheless, the guy was peeved at being caught out.

Teeth gritted, arm raised, he displayed no hesitation in firmly and decisively rendering his old pard *hors de combat*. The gun barrel laid across Cole's head effectively terminated any further resistance, much to the relief of his assailants. Any consolation Cole might have derived from having left them bloodied and battered from the set-to was of little consequence under the circumstances.

The attackers were breathing hard, thankful that the brutal fracas was over. None of them had anticipated such forceful resistance. Debris lay all around them. They could now readily appreciate why Randle had brought in the Kingpin. He had been no pushover, as their bruised faces and skinned knuckles testified.

Santee stood over the supine body, greatly tempted to deliver a solid boot to the exposed ribs. Such a cowardly urge, however, was resisted. He could unquestionably empathize with his old pal. Cole had only acted like any man worthy of the name.

'OK you guys, get him outside and on a horse,' Santee brusquely ordered. 'And make sure he's tied up good and tight. Then we'll take him up to that abandoned cabin in Dutchman's Draw.' That was when he noticed the cowering figure of the store-keeper. A stiff arm grasped the guy by the throat and half dragged him over the counter. 'One word about this to anyone and I'll be back,' he hissed.

The implied threat to his own continued good health needed no further elaboration for Ivor Webb, who was only too eager to conform. His spare frame trembled uncontrollably when the gang along with their comatose prisoner finally left the store. The only answer was a stiff belt of whiskey from the bottle kept below the counter. Another quickly followed before the trader's palpitating heart managed to regain its regular beat.

He slumped into a seat morosely surveying the damage caused by the fight. It would be left for him to clear up the mess knowing that his own pocket would suffer the consequences of paying for the damage. Yet perhaps he could glean something from this catastrophe. A malicious glint appeared in Webb's beady eye. Grabbing a hold of the signed list, he added an extra charge at the bottom for restitution, in the doubtful event that the drive did succeed.

Ivor Webb was not the only person who had beheld the abduction. Elly Clifford had just finished loading the supplies into the wagon out back when the fight broke out. The noise inside the store was a cogent warning to the girl that their clandestine plan had been discovered. She hurried inside peeping through the stockroom door, which was slightly ajar. What she beheld was sickening to the eye.

A hand covered her mouth to prevent the scream that threatened to reveal her presence. Much as she yearned to dive in and help the man whom she had once held in contempt, common sense held her back. What could she do against these hardened braggarts? Bulging eyes could only watch and hope for an early end to the awful torment. This rapid shift in fortunes had brought home a stark truth.

Eleanor was forced to acknowledge that she had unwittingly developed strong feelings for this man, feelings that pre-empted her earlier disdain. It was a startling discovery that could not be denied. Ever since that first meeting on the stagecoach, she knew that the seed had been sown. Now he was in big trouble, and all she could do was look on impotently.

Once the men had left with their battered and bruised captive, Eleanor glumly returned to the wagon in the rear alley. What could she do now to help Cole Jardine? Head bowed, sitting on the bench seat of the wagon, she surrendered to a bout of tears. But crying would not help. There had to be some more practical way of turning the tables on those thugs. Being raised on a cattle ranch with all its attendant problems, the girl had learned the hard lesson that God only helped those who helped themselves. It was a tough maxim, but accurate.

And then it came to her, a flash of inspiration. The leader of the assailants had let slip where they were going to incarcerate their prisoner. And Dutchman's Draw was on the way back to where the herd was corralled. This was her chance to rescue him. Turning the wagon around, Eleanor took a back trail that merged with the main one a mile south of Red Mesa. Before reaching the entrance to the Draw, she steered the wagon behind a cluster of rocks. And there she settled down to wait.

Time passed slowly. The night chill gripped her bones. She pulled a coat around her slim frame. A fire was out of the question. She had to remain hidden until the gang had done their worst and were returning to deliver the good news to Kez Randle. With the Kingpin safely incarcerated in Dutchman's Draw and out of the picture, the cattle drive would be leaderless and without supplies. The glum expression coating her downy features hardened. Well, that was going to change. She, Elly Clifford, would soon wipe that unctuous smile off'n his smarmy face.

Unfortunately for Waco Santee, in the heat of the moment he had overlooked the presence of the girl who had met Cole at the Yellow Dog. And that would be his undoing. Two hours seemed like ten as she waited, nervously praying that the gang had not finished him off with a bullet in the head. The Draw was well removed from any interference, a perfect hideout to remove the one obstacle to Kez Randle's odious plan for land acquisition.

She was nodding off when the sound of approaching hoof beats jerked her into wakefulness. All senses attuned to fever pitch, she huddled beside the concealed wagon gently stroking the muzzles of the horses to keep them calm. A single whinny at this stage could ruin everything. The steady drumming grew louder and louder before steadily fading as the riders passed on their way, ignorant of her presence.

An owl hooted in the distance, the throaty yelp of a coyote calling to its mate. Both were comforting sounds that enthused her confidence. Yet still she waited until silence descended over the lonely terrain. Moonlight filtered down through scattered cloud bolls littering the night sky.

TEN

. . . AND RESCUED!

An ethereal glow illuminated the way forward as she urged the wagon team back onto the trail. Dutchman's Draw was soon reached, its gloomy confines shutting out any light cast by the white watcher above. She was forced to let the horses pick their own route along the narrow fissure, which was only just wide enough to accommodate a wagon. Clumps of spiny mesquite brushed against the wooden sides. Luckily the Draw widened out after a couple of hundred yards.

Up ahead at the top end, a tiny flicker of light from a window indicated the position of the cabin. A lone horse was tied up outside. It appeared that only a single guard had been left to look after the prisoner. Eleanor now had to figure out some way of overcoming this obstacle. She paid little heed to the notion that being a woman was a hindrance in that respect.

In fact, it could be a distinct advantage. What man could resist helping a lady in distress?

Most Western males categorized women as 'good' or 'bad', the latter being dance hall gals and calico queens. A woman in trouble would arouse the macho image all men sought to espouse: that mythical knight in shining armour riding to the rescue of the damsel in distress. Eleanor smiled to herself, her teeth shone bright in the waxy corona cast by the moon. She couldn't fail.

Unhitching one of the horses, she led it forward to within hailing distance of the cabin. In the dark it would be hard for anybody to notice the fact that the animal lacked a saddle. Before laying down on the ground she checked that her pistol was loaded and functional. It was some time since she had fired it, and never previously in anger. The thought of having to do so produced a bubbling coat of sweat on her brow. The nervous reaction was brushed aside.

The tiny .32 calibre Wesson two-shot was in good order and fitted comfortably in her hand. She kept it with her at all times. Most of the time the Western frontier was an enchanting place in which to live. But it could also be very dangerous. Her father had taught her from an early age the rudiments of survival and self-protection that involved the use of firearms.

Sucking in a deep breath she called out in the most distressed voice she could muster, 'Help, help me, please. My horse has tripped and thrown me.' A convincing cry of pain added some much-needed authenticity to the charade.

Within less than a minute the door of the cabin opened and a bruiser known as Ira Bluecoat gingerly emerged. The said jacket was that of a Union sergeant from the 10th Ohio Regiment of Foot. It was ten years since the war had ended, but Bluecoat still insisted on wearing it. His gun was palmed and the wary critter was rightly displaying great caution. 'Who's out there? Show yourself if'n you don't want a bullet in the guts.'

Another bout of wailing was followed by the same angst-ridden plea for assistance. 'Help me please. I lost my way in the dark. My horse must have stepped in a gopher hole. I think my leg is broken.' More anguished yowling saw the burly tough holstering his pistol and hurrying down to where the girl was lying.

The horse stood some distance away munching on a clump of bunch grass. But Bluecoat only had eyes for the slender form seeking his help. This had never happened to the ugly critter before. One minute he was having to nursemaid that blamed gunslinger, the next this alluring prize had been thrown his way.

Bluecoat licked his thin lips, luridly anticipating the reward for aiding this powerless trophy. Any hesitation disappeared as he moved closer. The notion that he was being hoodwinked had dissolved like sugar in a coffee cup. The girl added her encouragement.

'Oh, thank you good sir for coming to my aid. I will be forever in your debt.' The glitter in the skunk's greed-filled eyes made her shiver as he drew closer.

105

Any second now and she would be ready to dispel his lust-filled notions. When he was no more than six feet away, Eleanor jumped to her feet producing the small pocket gun. 'One more step and you're dog meat, mister.' The blunt-edged snarl was completely at odds to the bleating wail of moments before.

Bluecoat was nonplussed, thrown by this sudden reversal of fortunes. Gone in an instant was his visualization of a lascivious paradise. Eleanor took full advantage of the thug's inertia. 'Hands in the air, and no sudden moves,' she snapped out firmly. 'This little beauty packs a heavyweight punch at close range.'

'You won't get away with this, sister,' the duped villain retorted. Now recovered from the shock of being hoodwinked by a dame, Bluecoat had no intentions of allowing this humiliating incident to end in her favour. He would have his way with her and then get rid of the body. If the boys ever found out what had really happened, he would become a laughing stock. That thought was enough to bring him to a standstill. The stiffly angular posture was a hint that compliance was out of the question.

'Shift your ass, you filthy dog,' Eleanor snapped, forcing herself to adopt the coarse language most likely to be heeded by this hard-nosed ruffian, yet not without some degree of foreboding. The catch in her throat betrayed the angst churning up her insides and making her gun hand tremble. Yet still she tried to maintain a resilient persona. 'What you waiting for?'

The sneaky varmint hawked out a macabre

chuckle. 'Nervous, ain't yuh missy? I can see it in your eyes, and hear the quake of fear in your voice. And so you ought to be.' A growl akin to that of a cornered mountain lion rumbled in the guy's throat. 'Nobody gets the better of Ira Bluecoat, especially not some dumb-assed piece of skirt.' He immediately threw himself to one side. His right hand grabbed for the holstered revolver.

The tiny Wesson belched out a thin tongue of flame, the slug chewing a hunk of leather from Bluecoat's boot heel. His own gun twisted to deliver its own invitation to the Reaper's party. But Eleanor kept her nerve, knowing she only had one more chance. The second bullet struck the braggart in the neck. Blood erupted from this savaging of the carotid artery. Bluecoat's mouth opened, flapping helplessly like a hooked trout. More of the red stuff spewed out like a hideously extended tongue as the man's life force quickly drained away.

All the girl could do was look on in horror at what she had done. She threw down the gun and sank to her knees stunned by the proximity of death in all its gruesome reality. She had witnessed the scythe man at work before – Indians, rustlers and the like – but never at such close quarters. And never by her own hand.

How long she remained there trying desperately to come to terms with what she had been forced to do, there was later no recollection. It was the snickering of her horse that brought her back to reality and the knowledge that Cole Jardine was still in that cabin.

But was he alive?

Not a sound had emerged from inside to indicate otherwise. Girding herself for the harsh truth, Eleanor approached the cabin with leaden feet. The door stood open. For a moment the gloom blurred her vision, not to mention the heinous reek, a blend of unwashed bodies, rancid fat and stale liquor.

Then she saw him, trussed up like a chicken ready for the oven and gagged to prevent any outburst. His head was caked in dried blood. The visible part of his face was bruised and swollen. He was barely conscious.

The girl emitted a heart-rending cry of anguish. Those cowardly braggarts had really given him a thorough going-over. He needed the expert ministrations of a sawbones. Eleanor was no nurse but she had been schooled by her mother in the basic essentials for the day-to-day running of a cattle ranch.

No further time was wasted on pointless recriminations. She untied him and hauled him up onto a grubby cot. With a damp cloth she wiped away the worst of the blood. Rheumy eyes flickered open, widening appreciably on seeing who was leaning over him. The smile made him wince as he tried to sit up.

'Don't move,' the girl ordered softly but firmly. 'We don't know how bad your injuries are yet.'

'Reckon it's almost worth the pain to have a nurse like you tending me,' he croaked out. 'You're a sight better to look on than that ugly cuss Bluecoat.' The chirpy twinkle dissolved as a stab of agony lanced through the battered frame. Gritted teeth and the manly need to appear strong and resilient held back the impulsive reaction to cry out. It took some minutes before the torment eased. The previous flippant manner was replaced by a grim resolve. 'If'n Randle thinks a few bruises are going to stop me completing this drive, he's tangling with the wrong man.'

Hot water and some horse liniment Elly found in a cupboard helped to cleanse the most serious lacerations. Luckily the injuries were superficial and would heal over time. Cole was thoroughly enjoying the tender care bestowed upon his battered frame. At the same time though, he was also anxious to hit the trail. But on that point, Elly was adamant. 'You're going to need a couple of days' rest before saddling up again.'

The patient grumbled but reluctantly conceded. Although he did not need much persuading. Only a jackass would baulk at being tended by such a delightful nurse. 'Only if'n I have your undivided attention at all times,' he blithely insisted.

'I ain't too sure about that,' Elly retorted adopting a lofty demeanour while secretly tingling at the prospect. She was still unsure of the direction in which her feelings for this man were heading. 'Jumble is the ranch medic. He won't take kindly to me muscling in on his territory.'

'I'm the boss now,' Cole averred, playing along with this enjoyable banter. 'So he'll do as I tell him.'

Hot food and a good night's rest found the invalid much restored by morning. His body felt stiff as a ramrod and ached all over. It was clear that he would not be charging around at the gallop for a couple more days. Nevertheless he was ready to ride and eager to get back to organizing the drive. All the stampeded cattle ought to have been rounded up by now and be ready to roll.

More serious, however, was the poignant observation submitted to his enchanting carer. 'Randle is sure to send someone over here to check that his prisoner remains out of action. Sooner we're out of here the better.'

'I hadn't thought of that,' Elly responded anxiously. 'It's less than an hour's ride to Red Mesa. We need to get moving.'

With Elly sitting up front handling the team, she insisted that Cole rest up inside the covered wagon. Any objections were squashed when it was pointed out that his presence on the bench seat would be more of a hindrance than a help. 'I need to concentrate on the horses,' she rightly contended, settling him onto some blankets in the bed of the wagon surrounded by the fresh supplies. 'In your present condition, you could easily fall off.'

By mid morning, they had arrived back at the holding ground where Ed Clifford was on tenterhooks. 'Where in tarnation have you been? It shouldn't have taken all this time to get those supplies. I was just about to send out a search party.'

Elly cut short her father's concerned outburst as she helped the injured Cole Jardine down from the wagon. 'It's a long story, Dad. I'll tell you about it later.' Right then there were more important issues at stake. 'Have the boys rounded up all the strays?' A curt nod from the disturbed rancher brought a sigh of relief. 'Then let's get this show on the road.'

But first there was one vital point that needed confirming. And it was stated by the cook. 'Pardon me Miss Elly, but did you manage to get those supplies?'

The girl smiled. 'Every single item on your list, Jumble. We sure won't be living on stringy rabbit and refried beans no more.' A cheer from the gathered cowboys greeted this most welcome of announcements. A ranch crew always worked much better on a full stomach prepared by a cook who knew his onions.

Clifford wasted no time in idle speculation. 'OK men, you heard the lady. Let's head 'em up and move 'em out!' This was the cry that enthuses all trail drivers. Whoops of delight rang out as the crew departed, each to his allotted job. Once again they were doing what they knew best, all eager to play their part.

Within the hour the drive was underway. Cole gingerly mounted his horse, stifling pained grimaces caused by the jolting motion. No way was he going to ride in the chuck wagon now. He would grin and bear it for his own self-esteem if nothing else. But he did hand over temporary management of the drive to Ed Clifford until such time as he felt ready to resume full control. A silent promise was made that it would not be later than the following day.

The lowing of cattle on the move, the jingle of saddle tack along with shouts of encouragement from riders were familiar sounds; sounds that lent a sense of comradeship and routine that was reassuring. Smoothly and with practised dexterity, the men slipped into the age-old ritual of the cattle drive.

Two men riding point moved to the front of the herd with a couple of flankers in the middle. There was only one drag rider to push the cattle along from the rear. This was the dustiest job but would be swapped around each day. Idaho Blue had elected to take over as horse wrangler in tribute to his dead pal. Being the hand who knew the trail better than anybody, Dan Mather rode ahead to scout the best route.

And so the drive was at last on the move. Normally a rate of around fifteen miles a day would be maintained. Following the unforeseen delays, Cole was aware that this was not enough if they were to reach Fort Belvedere within the stipulated time frame. He was itching to make his presence felt. Only his aching body held him back. Not to mention the ever-watchful supervision of Eleanor Clifford. Not that he was objecting to her presence.

The girl sensed his impatience to get back into the fray. 'Leave any of the heavy stuff until tomorrow, Cole, otherwise you'll regret it.' Her words of wisdom articulated in that silky voice were all that kept him in check. 'Have a little patience and we'll all reap the benefits.'

Dan Mather cut across to intercept the girl. His was the only face that failed to display a buoyant feeling of optimism. And he was now able to express his concerns without that darned interloper sticking his nose in. 'I reckon you're spending too much time bothering about Jardine,' he blurted out recklessly. 'Where do I stand in your affections? It ain't right, Elly. You're supposed to be marrying me.'

The girl squared her narrow shoulders, an imperious eye pinning the guy down. 'Is that so?' The sarcastic inflection was lost on the simple cowhand. 'And when did I agree to all this?'

'When you kissed me that time at Marlin's barn dance,' he shot back with an equal degree of asperity. 'You didn't object then.'

'Well I do now!' she snapped, pushing him away when he reached across to embrace her. 'That was then, and this is now. And I've never given you any hint that marriage was on the cards.'

'I took it for granted that was the trail we were following,' the aggrieved man bleated. 'I always thought you felt the same. It's that blasted hired gunslinger who has turned you against me.'

'It's you that's taken too much for granted, Dan. Nobody, neither you nor Cole Jardine, is going to tell me what's in my best interests.' And with that snappy rejoinder she walked away leaving the foreman downhearted. Although a cold leer told of anger burning within. A seething resentment that only needed a spark to ignite a conflagration greater than that from which they had so recently escaped.

ELEVEN

WACO STRIKES BACK

Heads turned as the rider galloped down the main street of Red Mesa and skidded to an ungainly halt outside the Yellow Dog. Poke Adderley leapt off his horse in a cloud of dust and hurried inside the saloon. He had ridden hard all the way back from Dutchman's Draw. 'Is the boss around?' he snapped out to the barman while hustling over to stairs.

'Him and that hired gunslinger are having a pow-wow in the office,' the guy replied, startled by the minder's rasping tone. 'But he gave orders not to be disturbed.'

'He'll want to hear this,' Adderley shot back, taking the steps two at a time. At the end of the cor-ridor he rapped on the office door and without waiting, barged straight in.

114

'What in thunderation are you doing busting in here like you own the place?' Randle blasted angrily. 'It better be good.'

The sweating roughneck barely paused to draw breath as he blurted out, 'Jardine has escaped from the cabin. He must have somehow broke free.'

'What about Bluecoat?' asked Randle, trying to get his head around this unwelcome piece of news. 'He was meant to be guarding the skunk.'

'Shot dead. I found him outside the cabin.' Adderley scratched his chin offering a puzzled frown. 'But one thing I don't get. He was shot with a .32 bullet. It looked like one of those prissy little popguns done for him.'

'Those things are only carried by women,' remarked the gambler with an equally confused frown.

It was Santee who provided the answer to the conundrum. He slammed a bunched fist into the palm of his hand as the truth dawned. 'It must have been that Clifford dame. I forgot all about her. She must have followed us to the Draw.'

Randle's face darkened, the thick eyebrows knitting in anger. 'I ain't paying you to make a mess of things. You should have killed him while you had the chance.' An accusatory look drilled into the hired gunnie. 'You ain't going soft on the bastard I hope just cos you know each other.'

Santee vehemently spurned the allegation. 'I accepted this job and I'll see it through to the end. That dame cottoning on to our plan was a mistake

115

anyone could make. But mark my words, he won't get the better of Waco Santee a second time.'

Randle simmered down, apparently mollified by the explanation. Although he was none too impressed that the renowned gunslinger was free, and he was now a man down. 'With Jardine back in the fray, you'll need to act quickly. By now they'll have rounded up the cattle and be ready to start the drive.'

'Which route will they take?' Santee enquired, not being familiar with the area.

'You're from round these parts.' Randle said addressing Rube Thurman. 'Which way do you think they'll go?'

The hardcase evinced no hesitation with his reply. 'Only one way to go. Straight down the valley following the Gunnison until it bends east. Then round the edge of the Spruce Mountains along Delta Creek. Keeping up a steady pace, it should take around two weeks to reach Fort Belvedere if'n they push hard enough.'

Santee paced up and down the room, his brain working hard to figure out a weak spot that he could exploit. 'What's the terrain like once they leave the Gunnison?' he asked Thurman.

Perked up that his local knowledge was required, the minder was anxious to accredit himself with distinction. It was a rarity for his opinion to be sought out and he intended to take full advantage of this chance to impress the boss. 'My bet is that they'll head down a branch valley called the Uncompagre. It's steep-sided and bordered by rocky outcrops. But the valley has good grass. Only problem they'll face is a head wind that funnels along from the south.'

Santee's eyes lit up. 'That's where we'll hit them,' he articulated briskly. 'And this time, I'll make darned certain it's the end of the line.'

Within a half hour, Santee was leading his men out of Red Mesa. Alongside him rode Rube Thurman. Tall in the saddle, eager to impress his sidekicks with the newfound status, he spurred his horse ahead. Barely noticeable from the main trail, the cocky tough branched off along a thin track to take a short cut across the Montrose Plateau. When questioned by Santee as to the efficacy of the detour, he confidently declared that it would bring them out ahead of the cattle drive.

All day they rode climbing steadily through stands of pine and fir, crossing wild terrain that rarely witnessed the passage of human travellers. Thurman exhibited no hesitation in his choice of route as they passed through a labyrinth of rocky canyons. 'You sure this is gonna work, Rube?' Santee edgily enquired on more than one occasion.

The smug villain shrugged off the gunman's concerns. 'I used to trap beaver pelts in these hills afore silk-lined hats became all the rage for them city gents,' Thurman replied with a surly curl of the lip. 'Those were the good times.' His eyes misted over as past recollections loomed large in his imagination. 'Me and the other trappers enjoyed many a rousing shindig at the rendezvous up on the Green River. But all good things come to an end. They call it progress and there's no going back. Don't make it right though.' Thurman shut down, clearly saddened by the passing of an era in which he had been an active participant.

That night they camped in a small glade beside a trickling creek. Poke Adderly caught a couple of large trout while another guy called Ezra Pound shot a small deer. Over coffee laced with generous measures of whiskey the ex-fur trapper regaled them with ribald incidents from his past life. For a moment the grim reality of their mission was forgotten.

All too soon they were back in the saddle as the golden orb raised its head above the scalloped moulding of Iron Mountain. Thurman pointed to the distinctive peak. 'On the west side is the Columbine Pass,' he boldly asserted. 'A half day's ride beyond and we'll be into the Uncompagre with a day to spare.' The secure smile gave the others a trust in their buddy's competence, further buoying his own self-belief.

And so it proved. Santee was well satisfied and heaped praise on the preening Thurman. It was late on the next day that Ezra Pound reported back that the herd had just entered the eastern end of the Uncompagre.

Santee gave the news a malicious grin. 'Get those torches alight, boys. And make sure the whole valley goes up in smoke. Once this grass is burnt to a crisp, there's no way they can push cattle this way. They'll be finished. And we can all collect those bonuses promised by the boss.'

That was news each of the men welcomed wholeheartedly. As soon as all the torches were alight Santee ordered the men to spread themselves across the valley. Poke Adderley had been sent to keep a lookout for the approaching herd. 'Don't set the grass alight until I get the word from Poke,' Santee ordered the others. 'We need this fire to spread out as a single conflagration.'

It was the fifth day of the cattle drive and so far everything was progressing according to plan. The scouts had reported no sign of any unwelcome visitors. Cole and Ed Clifford were watching the passage of the herd from a low knoll. 'Keep this up and we'll be at Fort Belvedere well ahead of schedule,' Clifford remarked brightly. He pointed to a break in the valley up ahead. 'That's where we branch off. The Uncompagre has good grass which will keep the cattle fattened up, enabling the boys to push them harder. We should be able to do twenty miles a day through there.'

Cole was less confident than his associate. 'I wouldn't be so sure, Ed.' A dubious gaze, dark as the night sky, swung contemplating the new valley as the prospect of resistance loomed large in his mind's eye. 'With my old partner Waco Santee on his payroll, Randle ain't gonna just sit tight and give us a free hand. We'll need to keep all our wits about us. From now on I want the night guard doubled.'

Two more days passed and they had just branched off along the Uncompagre. But Cole's notion that problems redolent of human skulduggery lay ahead wavered not a jot. 'I'm going ahead to scout the lie of the land,' he told the foreman.

'Do you want me to circle the herd for the night?' Mather asked, expectant of a halt being called. But he was sadly mistaken.

'There's still a couple of hours' daylight,' came back the crisp rejoinder. 'Keep those longhorns moving at a good lick.'

'The boys have been going all day and everyday. They need some sleep,' Mather complained.

'Quit your griping,' Cole snapped back acidly. 'It seems to be all you ever do. And you tell the boys they can sleep 'til Thanksgiving once we get to Fort Belvedere.'

Mather hesitated, scowling, all set to argue the toss. The rock solid glare from Cole Jardine effectively crushed any opposition proposed. Tossing off a surly grunt, the foreman swung his mount off and galloped away.

That fella and me are gonna cross swords in the none too distant future, Cole surmised as he turned and headed up the valley. Two miles into the Uncompagre, the valley bent away to the left in a wide arc. Immediately beyond, it narrowed to little more than twenty yards. Turrets of red sandstone on either side forced the potential trail down to little more than a narrow fissure. It was only a hundred yards long. But this was where the expected resistance poured forth in all its rampant fury.

Smoke billowed out of the gorge. On the far side, Cole could hear shouts as men lit more fires across

120

the trail. Even as he watched in horrified awe, flames burst from the restrictive flue fanned by a stiff wind, made all the more potent by the funnelling influence. Orange tentacles reached out devouring every blade of grass in their path. Dark clouds of dense smoke obscured the late afternoon sun and every other landmark. Cole scowled, gritting his teeth. So this was what those varmints had in mind all along. They must have cut across country to head them off.

There was no time to lose if the herd was to be saved. Even so, with the fire moving at such a fast rate, it would be touch and go. Galloping back like the devil was on his tail, Cole pushed his horse to the limit. It was lucky he had only come two miles. Waving his hat frantically to attract attention, he yelled out for the herd to be turned. 'There's a prairie fire heading this way down the valley. It'll swallow us up if'n we don't get those beasts across the river. Move your asses, boys. This is a matter of life and death.'

The next hour was a frantic scramble to guide the herd back down the Uncompagre and across Delta Creek. Half that time had been spent in turning them gently to prevent another stampede. No easy task when time was against them. But the experience of Mather and his men saved the day. The last of the herd was wading across the broad reach of Delta Creek just as the first flames were licking at their heels.

Thankfully the shallow watercourse was wide enough to prevent the fire spreading. Camp was made on the far bank. Cole and the rest of crew could only stand and watch morosely as the raging inferno slowly burnt itself out. It looked to all intents and purposes as if the Flying C cattle drive had been well and truly scuppered.

But the Kingpin was not beaten yet. Somehow he would get the herd to market, of that he was determined. As the men were settling the jumpy cattle down, Cole lit up a stogie and looked across at the angry flames on the far side of the creek. The fiery red arms appeared almost lifelike, waving frantically in frustration at having been denied their prey.

It had been a close-run thing. There was no sign of the skunks who had started the blaze. Cole was in no doubt, however, that Waco Santee was the instigator. No doubt his old pard was at that very moment reporting the success of his mission back to Kez Randle.

'Well I ain't beaten yet,' he snarled under his breath. 'One way or another, I'll beat you to the punch, Randle.'

Next morning, Cole had the men up bright and early. In stark contrast to the previous day when an upbeat sense of sanguinity had imbued their disposition, the men were now downcast and in low spirits. The drive was over; they had been beaten. There would be no payout after all. Glum expressions greeted the boss when he gathered them together after breakfast. His order to get the herd ready for continuing the drive were met with startled looks of scepticism and much grunting.

As expected, Dan Mather was the first to voice his objections. 'You're crazy to think we can move the herd up the Uncompagre. They'd choke to death on the ash.'

Cole stepped up to the guy, thrusting out a craggy jaw. In a low yet compelling hiss, he poked Mather in the chest to emphasize his antipathy. 'That's the second time you've brought my sanity into dispute. It won't happen a third time.' His hand stroked the butt of the Peacemaker. The intimation was clear. 'And to relieve you of any concern, I'm not going that way.'

'There ain't no other way,' Mather sneered. 'You'll have to turn back.'

'That's where you're wrong,' Cole countered. 'I have no intention of letting Kez Randle win. So I've decided to take them over the mountains.'

The universal reaction to this startling revelation was a wholesale babble of negative comments. 'It can't be done,' Mather spat out, vehemently conveying what everybody else felt, including Ed Clifford. 'I know that country and nobody has ever taken a herd over there before.'

'Well I'm gonna be the first.'

Mather stood his ground. 'You really are crazy if'n you think we'll follow you over that wilderness. It's a suicide mission.'

Without another word, Cole's right arm shot out. It was a solid blow and bang on the button. Mather fell backwards. Lying on his back, the victim's right hand reached for his own pistol.

'Draw that hogleg and you're a dead man,' Cole

rasped. He made no attempt to go for his own holstered .45. But the foreman knew he could never outdraw the infamous Kingpin. All he could do was cuss impotently.

He scrambled to his feet rubbing an aching jaw. 'You figure I'm gonna help after that?' he ranted. 'No chance, mister.' His next blunt comment was to the watching hands. 'You guys want to work for this mad man, that's your lookout. I ain't that stupid. I'm pulling out.'

'You've gotten five minutes to gather up your gear and skedaddle.' Cole's revolver jumped into his hand. 'Then I'll let my equalizer do the talking.' The time limit found the estranged foreman disappearing in a cloud of dust. 'So what's it to be, men?' Cole addressed the remaining cowboys. 'You guys ready to achieve the impossible? In my view, nothing is impossible until somebody's given it a try. And what have you got to lose?'

'Only our lives,' piped up a hand called Red Stiller. The others muttered and grumbled, nodding heads concurring with the macabre sentiment. The continuance of the drive was now teetering on a knife edge.

It was left for Ed Clifford to drag them back from the brink. He moved over, standing beside the new owner of the Flying C to show his support. 'I'm willing to take that chance if'n you boys are,' he averred briskly. 'And they tell me that its mighty pretty country up there at this time of year, health-giving as well. So what do you say? Are you with us?'

Chuckles greeted this piece of wholesome acumen,

the tension noticeably easing. As the new unelected spokesman for the hands, Red Stiller stepped forward. 'Me and the boys reckon if'n you think it can be done, Mr Clifford, then we're ready to back you all the way.'

Cole heaved a sigh of relief. 'Then pack up your gear and let's get moving.' As the men dispersed Cole turned to the old rancher. 'I'm much obliged to you, Ed. That was touch and go there.'

'It's in all our interests to get these steers to Fort Belvedere on time.' Clifford offered a half smile, winking at the younger man. 'Those guys just needed a friendly push in the right direction. Always remember, son. Men work a lot harder if'n they feel appreciated. A word of praise here and there works wonders for morale.'

'Guess I still have a lot to learn,' sighed Cole.

'You're getting there. And you have grit and fortitude, which is half the battle in this country. And you're gonna need that in bucketfuls over the next couple of weeks if'n we're to succeed.'

TWELVE

TURNCOAT

Waco Santee was enjoying a celebratory drink in the Yellow Dog with Kez Randle. Both men were admiring the entertainment on stage provided by singer Lily Devine supported by a troupe of exotic dancers. 'That was a good plan of your'n, allowing a fire to do all the hard work,' Randle commended the hired gunman. 'You are certain they can't go through that valley once it's burned itself out?'

Santee scoffed at the suggestion. 'Any fool attempting to push beef across that burnt-out cinder patch will find himself with a thousand head of dead carcases. Cattle on the move need constant graze. They don't have the sense not to eat the ash. And it'll choke up their gullets. Any cattleman knows that.' The gunman filled up his glass. 'That herd ain't going no place 'cept back down the valley.'

Satisfied that the Flying C was almost within his

grasp, Randle sat back to enjoy the show. Santee was thinking what all that dough was going to buy him. Perhaps he would go down the trail favoured by his old partner and buy a spread of his own. And with Lily as lady of the house, life couldn't get much better.

The one fly in the ointment was the Kingpin. Cole wouldn't sit by and allow a setback like this to pass with impunity. Sooner or later, a showdown between the two old buddies seemed inevitable. Unless of course he could get in first. Brow furrowed in thought, he failed to observe the arrival of Dan Mather. First he knew of the guy's presence was when he sat down opposite, addressing himself to Randle.

The gambler was not best pleased to have one of the enemy setting down uninvited. 'What in tarnation do you want?' he snorted. A raised hand saw numerous tough-looking jaspers closing in on the lone figure. 'The Yellow Dog is a mighty dangerous place for a critter working against my interests.'

Mather discounted the encircling minders while shrugging off Randle's intimidation. He had a proposition the saloon owner would be foolish to ignore. 'I've quit the Flying C. That's why I'm here. To offer you my services,' he claimed. Lowered eyes focused on the whiskey bottle in the middle of the table.

'Go ahead. You look like you need a drink,' Randle consented. 'What could you possibly have that I would want?' The assertion was spiked with irony. 'Thanks to Mr Santee here, that herd is going nowhere. All I have to do now is wait until the end of the month and claim my due when Jardine can't repay the loan.' Mocking eyes matched the curled lip as Randle leaned back in his chair.

Mather tipped back the glass and drank deep. The bite of hard liquor bolstered his self-assurance. He leaned forward knowing he now had the whip hand. And he intended to make the most of his advantage. His opening remark was to Santee.

'You were right in figuring that a range fire would prevent the herd moving down the Uncompagre. We only just managed to get it back across Delta Creek.' He paused to give added credence to the punch line.

Randle was becoming impatient. 'Don't tell us what we already know. The boys are getting edgy to deliver some of the medicine meted out to Jardine before the skunk escaped from Dutchman's Draw. I hope for your sake you weren't in on that. We're all mighty sore about losing Ira Bluecoat.'

'Not a chance.' Mather hawked out a mirthless laugh. 'I wouldn't lift a blamed finger to help that piece of dog shit.'

The snide remark saw Santee stiffening. Cole and he might be on opposing sides in this caper, but that didn't mean he didn't still rate the guy. A restraining hand on his arm cooled the instinct to retaliate.

'Let the guy have his say,' Randle advanced. 'If'n I don't cotton to his suggestion, he's all your'n. OK, fella, let's have it.'

Still Mather couldn't resist another sly dig. 'He sure didn't look like no big shot gunslinger when he arrived back at camp. As for what I can offer you, how about this?' Another grinning pause for effect. 'Jardine ain't about to give up. He aims to take the herd over the Spruce Mountains.'

That bolt from the blue dumbfounded the gambler. His mouth fell open, black eyes bulging wide as saucers. Finally he found his voice. 'Can it be done?'

'Only someone desperate enough would attempt such a crazy trip,' Mather suggested with measured restraint. 'But with luck on his side and determination, it's just about possible.'

'If'n Cole says he's gonna cross those mountains, he'll do it, or die trying,' Santee interrupted. 'That guy don't know the meaning of "can't be done".'

'Then its up to you to stop him,' Randle growled, his previous apprehension now under control. 'Remember the balance of your fee only gets paid when I take possession of the ranch. Take all the boys along. Mather knows that country so he can guide you.'

'Just so long as he keeps ahead of me.' Santee regarded the turncoat with a supercilious glower. 'I'm like Cole. I don't cotton to backshooters.'

Mather chewed his lower lip but held himself in check. He was in the lion's den. One false move could be his last. His main concern was to avenge himself on that self-righteous gunslinger who had stolen what he adjudged to be his bequest. And that did not only include the ranch. Eleanor appeared to have lost her heart to the lowdown critter. And there was only one answer to that. His hand stroked the gun on his hip.

For the initial few days the cattle drive proved surprisingly straightforward. The gradient into the foothills rose steadily but without any insurmountable obstacles to stall their progress. The men were buoyed up and morale was the highest it had been for some time. But Cole knew that the most testing phase lay ahead of them. This would be no Sunday school picnic.

Pine and aspen predominated the landscape. Interspersed with dangerous rocks the blend made herding that much more difficult. The trees were also blocking out the route ahead. All Cole knew was that they needed to maintain a south-westerly course as near as possible. He prayed that he had done the right thing in making this hazardous expedition into virgin territory. But what other choice had he been given?

The further into the mountain wilderness they ventured, the tougher the going became. Other than thin deer runs there were no trails; thick undergrowth made it hard for the drovers to maintain control over the herd. Then on the fifth day, another serious issue arose. Cole had been enjoying a much-needed mug of coffee when Whiskey Joe galloped up. 'We gotten a problem, boss,' he gasped out.

Cole waited for the rannie to elucidate. 'Wolves!' That single word was enough to strike fear into those within earshot. 'There's a pack of them up in the hills. They caught one of the calves and stripped it down to the bone. Those critters must be mighty hungry.'

More used to dealing with two-legged predators, Cole called on Ed Clifford for his opinion. 'Only way is to lure them out of hiding so we can shoot them down. Best chance of that is to offer up a decoy. Tether another calf in the open and conceal ourselves nearby. Then, all we can do is wait it out. Might take a while. But if'n what Joe says is true and they're hungry, we won't have long to hang around.'

And so it proved. The pack emerged that night, slinking round the edge of the clearing with teeth bared. Slaver dribbled from their muzzles in anticipation of the imminent feast. Six pairs of eyes glowed red as they prepared to commence the attack. A large critter, bigger than all the rest and clearly the leader made the first move. In a single bound he launched himself at the terrified calf. In mid flight three bullets struck him in the body. Flashes of orange spat out from the concealing rocks as the defenders quickly finished off the rest of the pack.

'Well done, boys,' Cole praised his crew. 'Reckon we all deserve a break after that set-to.' He called across to a cowboy called Banjo Rudd. 'Let's have a bit of music. And pass those candy bars around that I was saving, Jumble. Nothing like a good singsong around the campfire to set us up for the new day.'

Clifford smiled as his daughter sat down beside the young rancher. 'You're learning, boy,' he muttered to himself.

THIRTEEN

FLYING HIGH

Next day everything quickly reverted to the normal hard grind. Frequent use was made of the compass Cole had inherited from his father. The elder Jardine had scouted for the army up in Montana before retiring. It was a much-prized possession that offered a constant reminder that he had not seen the old guy for more than three years. When this was all over, he promised himself a trip north, perhaps even with a new bride. Although that assumption was still up in the air.

As height was gained so the temperature dropped. The men needed to don their fleece coats and angora chaps. Snow could be seen on the distant peaks. Even in summer it never entirely disappeared. Cole wondered if their passage would involve traversing the white stuff. It seemed more than likely unless

132

they could navigate a lower route through the mountains.

With height also came steep descents and detours to avoid impossible acclivities. Scouts were sent ahead to check the lie of the land and report back any arduous sections. The pace slowed measurably as the terrain became rougher. The cowboys needed to keep the steers bunched to avoid any straying over cliff edges.

It was inevitable, unfortunately, that some would be lost. Broken legs and tumbles accounted for a few. Cole knew that he could not afford to lose too many. Accepting the advice of those with more experience of cattle drives, especially Ed Clifford, he urged the men to be vigilant and constantly on their guard. He was particularly anxious about any betrayal from Dan Mather.

During that night's lay over on a rare piece of flat ground in one of the mountain valleys, he stated his concerns to the older man. They were sat round the campfire enjoying a convivial smoke over a cup of coffee.

'That guy has more than likely hotfooted straight back to Red Mesa and offered his services to Randle,' he glumly remarked to Clifford.

Eleanor was listening in. She balked at the suggestion. 'Dan would never betray us in that way,' she protested. 'His loyalty has always been to the Flying C.'

'I wouldn't be so sure, honey,' her father said, adding his support. 'That was before Cole here came

133

along. He was mighty peeved at losing face in front of the men. And there are other reasons too.' He didn't need to name them.

'That's a load of hogwash,' she disputed, knowing exactly to what her father was referring.

'Is it?' The gentle probing of her spirited denial caused Eleanor's face to visibly redden. To avoid any further discomfiture or inquest into her feelings, she stalked off to help Jumble with the preparation of supper.

'Don't worry, son,' the old rancher appeased his solemn companion. 'She'll come round. But you're gonna have to eat some humble pie. Elly's a tough cookie who knows her own mind. She gets that from her ma. Women brought up on the frontier have to be. It's a hard life. But I seen the way she looks at you.' He smiled. 'You just make sure to push the herd through to Fort Belvedere. Then we can all relax and start enjoying the good life again.'

'First thing tomorrow, I'll send one of the hands back to keep a watch out for any pursuit,' Cole declared. 'Now that he's got Waco and likely Mather as well on his payroll, Randle is sure to try something and I intend to be ready when he does.'

'That's good thinking,' Clifford agreed. 'Since you arrived on the scene, Dan has shown his true colours. I reckon Elly has had a lucky escape.'

And so the drive progressed. But it was getting tougher by the day, even the hour. The terrain became noticeably more broken, the grass diminishing in quantity as well as quality. It was hardest for the chuck wagon, which was lagging behind. Extra horses from the remuda were needed to provide enough hauling power to the converted conestoga. They could not afford to lose it down one of the numerous ravines, cliff edges and boulder fields that constantly threatened its survival.

Crunch time arrived when the wagon finally reached the zenith of its journey. A gap had been scouted through the mountains. The cattle had already negotiated a stone-choked gully, plunging headlong down a steep 200-foot slope into the level valley floor below. It had been touch and go. The hands needed all their experience and acumen to prevent the bawling beasts from trampling each other in the narrow cleft. With skill and dexterity they achieved the near impossible.

The wagon was left teetering on the lip of the downfall. Jumble categorically refused to go any further. When challenged by Cole to shift his damned ass, the stubborn cook expressed his chagrin in no uncertain terms. 'The wagon will be smashed to bits, and me along with it. No way am I putting my life on the line going down there.'

It was indeed a mind-boggling descent. But there was no other way forward. And with time against them, Cole was adamant that he was not for turning back. 'We can't afford to waste time searching for another route if'n that deadline is gonna be met,' he espoused as Clifford and the drag riders gathered round. 'This is the only way forward. We have to find a way down.'

It was Banjo Rudd who provided the answer. 'We could chop down a couple of pine trunks and tether them to the rear of the wagon. They will act as a break and keep it from running away and crashing.'

Cole immediately approved the scheme. Axes were produced, and they set to work with a will. The dull thud of steel on wood echoed through the densely packed phalanx of trees. Sharp blades urged on by straining muscles soon had a pair of hefty logs roped up to the rear of the wagon. Jumble was still exceedingly nervous about descending the acclivitous chute so Cole climbed up beside him and took the reins.

'All set?' he called out to the terrified cook. The frenzied leer from his boss was a reminder of the Grim Reaper and did nothing to enhance the poor guy's confidence. All he could do was grip the sides of the wagon tightly and pray for deliverance from this mad enterprise.

'Good luck, fellas,' Clifford shouted as all the hands joined in the enthusiastic cheering. A trembling nod saw Cole taking his boot off the brake lever and hollering out a manic howl to bolster his own spirit of bravado. The whip cracked over the heads of the horses urging them over the rim. In no time the wagon was bouncing and careering down the steep gully. Swaying perilously from side to side, every spin of the wheels threatened to unseat its two occupants.

The tremendous noise akin to a rampaging herd of buffalo went unheeded as Cole concentrated on maintaining control of the downhill stampede. His boot continually stamped hard on the brake lever causing a manic squealing that set his nerves on edge. Trees and outcrops of rock were passed in the blink of an eye.

At one point during the headlong dash, a large moose flashed across their bows, its antlers gleaming in the dappled sunlight filtering through the dense tree cover. A bark of disapproval merged with the general cacophony.

Just when Cole thought the worst was over, the wagon jolted leaping into the air as it struck a rocky projection. That would surely have sealed their fate had not the logs affixed to their rear steadied the wagon. Terra firma was gained in a thundering shudder that ought to have broken the wheels. But this was an old conestoga, built to withstand a deal of punishment. Ever onward they rushed, hurtling towards their destiny.

After what seemed like a hundred lifetimes, the end was in sight. As suddenly as it had begun the ground flattened out. The suicidal scurry was over. Those logs had effectively done their job. Without the heavy counter weights, the wagon would most certainly never have made it to the bottom in one piece, more like a thousand.

Cole slapped the leathers, wrestling the panic-stricken team to a juddering halt. Both riders breathed deep. That had been a close-run thing. 'Gee, boss, you sure know how to handle a team,' Jumble gushed, grateful still to be alive. 'That was one ride I don't want to repeat. Where did you learn that?'

A shake of the head was Cole's reply as dust rose in clouds around them. 'Never been up on a wagon before. That sure is a first for me. And hopefully a last. I'll leave the driving to you in future.'

The first person to reach the wagon was Eleanor Clifford. The concern in her ardent gaze sent shivers down Cole's spine. 'Are you all right?' she blurted out, grabbing his hand. It was an instinctive reaction. He was clearly unhurt, merely in a state of shock that soon dissipated as euphoria took over. The wagon had been saved; he had survived a desperate episode; and the drive could continue unabated. Such life-assuring truths paled into insignificance with the girl of his dreams now staring dreamily into his eyes and holding his hand. Pure paradise.

The magical moment was crushed. The bubble burst when a shout to their rear heralded the arrival of Whiskey Joe. The cowboy had been delegated to watch their rear in case of a pursuit.

He slithered to a halt beside the wagon. 'I counted a dozen riders about five miles back, boss,' the rannie called out. 'They've just crossed that creek with an island in the middle.' Cole recalled the hairy crossing the day before. 'They're headed this way. And guess what?' The jasper was bubbling to relate his news, but still couldn't resist a pause to grip his listeners. 'Dan Mather was leading them.'

This was something Cole had expected, but not so the assembled hands who muttered angrily amongst themselves. They had all respected the rugged foreman for his loyalty to Ed Clifford and the Flying

C. None could ever have predicted that he would become a turncoat, collaborating with the enemy.

'Why that double-crossing rat!' ejaculated Idaho Blue.

Eleanor gasped, barely able to accept the heinous truth. 'How could he do such a despicable thing?'

Her father was more perceptive. 'Didn't take him long to change sides,' he commented knowingly. 'Although it still hurts that he would turn on us like this.'

'It was always on the cards when he pulled out like that. And I reckon Waco Santee will be riding alongside him,' Cole added, quickly trying to work out the best course of action to take.

FOURTEEN

BOX OF TRICKS

Not being conversant with this wild terrain in the
heart of the Spruce Mountains, Cole was dependent
on any knowledge that could be supplied by his men.
They were all aware of the dire situation facing them.
With Randle's bunch of hijackers hot on their heels
there was no time to lose if they were to save the herd.
He walked away from the others, his brain working
overtime to figure out some way of defeating their
pursuers. His mind harked back to past times before
he and Waco had joined up.

And that was when the answer to his conundrum
slapped him in the face. A simple ruse that had
worked a treat up in Montana when he had been
working for a rancher called Elias Burk who owned
the Frying Pan ranch. Up there in the Big Belt

140

country he had been faced with a similar difficulty. On that occasion it had been a skunk with the odious handle of Crazy Clu Haggard. A heavyweight land grabber just like Kez Randle who wanted to take over the entire Musselshell Valley.

There was no reason why he couldn't pull the same stunt here. All he needed to find was the right terrain. Straight away he called the men together. 'You all know the score. Randle's men are on our tail. They'll catch us up sometime later today unless we can outfox them.' He looked at the cowboys, trying to gauge their reaction for partaking in the tough battle ahead. These guys were not hard-bitten gunnies. Would they be prepared to put their lives on the line? 'Any of you want to pull out now, I'll understand and there'll be no hard feelings.'

He waited on tenterhooks, expecting one or two at least to throw in the towel. Nobody moved. It was Red Stiller who voiced the universal mood. 'Most of us have been with the Flying C a long time. We ain't about to surrender the herd to a rat like Randle.' The gnarled features of a face weathered to resemble beaten leather cracked in a self-conscious smile. 'And there's that bonus at the end.'

The tension evident in Cole's stiff posture drained away. 'I'm more'n grateful, boys. You won't regret it. If'n we all pull together in what I have in mind, that dough will be in your pockets licketty spit, I promise.' Then he got down to the business of continuing the drive. 'We have the rest of the day to push these critters as far as possible. At least the terrain looks better from here on. Ed's in charge while I head off to seek out the right place to make our stand.'

He spurred off, praying that a suitable box canyon could be located into which to lure their adversaries. For an hour he followed the meandering course of the steep-sided upland valley. It swung between mountainsides cloaked in the dark green of pine. But that for which he was looking failed to materialize. No break in the endless massed ranks to indicate the presence of a box canyon.

No strength emanated from the sun. Up here the cold was intense. Luckily they were just below the snowline. He hunkered down into the fleece jacket to keep warm. Neither was there any sign of human occupation. Even the ubiquitous mountain trapper had forsaken this desolate spot. Birds flew overhead with the occasional sighting of deer in the distance. Chipmunks and cotton-tail rabbits were more common. So at least there was food.

Cole surmised that perhaps he was the first of his kind to tread this wild and remote land. If there had been more time he would have considered naming the various landmarks. But time was of the essence. He needed to find that canyon.

At least the general grade was starting to go steadily downward. So he must be nearing the end of this hair-raising expedition. No consolation if Santee and his gang caught them out in the open. He would give it another half hour. If nothing had presented itself by then, other plans would have to be concocted.

Then he saw it. The first cleft in the bleak land-scape. He swung his horse across the creek to the far side, negotiating huge boulders seemingly tossed down at random from the heights above. No cactus plants in this coldly remote place, only tough grass and low-lying shrubs. The distinctive aperture led into a separate wing about fifty yards across. He spurred to the far end, a distance of around a half mile. And lo and behold, it terminated in that all-important dead end. There was ample room for the herd to bed down. And some flat ground to make camp.

His eyes glittered with vengeful intent. Those varmints were going to receive the shock of their lives. Satisfied with his discovery and eager to relate the news to Ed Clifford, he wasted no time in hot-footing back down the valley to meet up with the approaching herd.

The urgency of their precarious situation had encouraged the drovers to push the steers to the limits of their endurance. Cole joined in the steady and unrelenting push forward not wishing to reveal his plan for the present. All that mattered was getting the herd bedded down in the box canyon before nightfall.

It was with some hesitancy that Clifford agreed to Cole's insistence that the herd be driven into what he reckoned was a trap. 'This is gonna lock us in with no way out,' he asserted, challenging the new rancher's decision. 'We need to be in the open to put up any decent resistance.'

143

'You agreed that I was in charge of this operation, right?' came back an equally forthright rejoinder. Ed gave a reluctant nod, wondering if'n the high country had affected the guy's brain cells. 'Well trust me then. I know what I'm doing.' Ed shrugged, turning away to issue orders for the herd to be pushed into the box canyon.

Light was fading fast by the time the last of the steers had been settled down for the night. Ed was preparing to set the night guard when Cole stopped him. 'No watch tonight. All the men will bed down around the campfire.'

This time, Clifford's opposition was firm. 'You gone plumb loco, boy? We'll be sitting ducks for any attackers.'

Eleanor was equally at odds with what appeared to be a scheme playing into the hands of their enemies. She was less vehement in her misgivings, but voiced them nonetheless. 'I can't see how bottling ourselves up like this can possibly help defeat a much stronger force.'

Cole chuckled, offering the bemused pair a crafty smile. 'That's the whole idea. Except that we won't be bunking down by the fire.'

He waited as Ed Clifford mulled over this conundrum, forehead wrinkling in thought before the true essence of the plan began to resolve itself. Cole helped out by heaving a sack of flour over to the fire and covering it with a blanket. He set down a hat on top. Clifford slapped his thigh. 'Well I'll be a horned toad!' he exclaimed. 'Why in thunder didn't I think of that? You're a genius, boy.'

'In my old line of work I've picked up a devious box of tricks along the way,' Cole nonchalantly conceded, accepting the compliment with a neat flourish. 'You never know when they might come in handy.'

The sun had dipped below the scabrous ridge line encircling the canyon when the bogus campers were finally settled around the blazing fire. 'Pile on more wood,' Cole ordered. 'We want those critters to have good targets to aim at when they attack.' Finally satisfied that all the 'sleeping drovers' were convincing in the flickering light, he said, 'Spread yourselves out in the surrounding rocks. And make sure your weapons are fully loaded. Anybody foolish enough to think the Flying C is finished is going to receive a bloody nose.'

There was no knowing when the pursuers would hit the camp. Or even if it would be during the hours of darkness. Although Cole felt sure that his old partner would prefer the night hours to enable him to launch a surprise attack. It was fortunate that the current ruse had been devised before Cole and Santee had teamed up otherwise the other man would almost certainly have sussed it out and acted accordingly by hanging back until daylight and blocking them into the canyon.

As things stood, he was confident that sooner or later during the next few hours, an attack would be launched. Time passed slowly. All the hands had been warned not to smoke or make any noise. The slightest hint of skulduggery would most surely kibosh the wily plot. The moon etched a slow path across the night sky.

'Do you think they'll fall for it?' Clifford whispered. He was not the most patient of guys. 'This waiting is getting on my nerves.'

'Sure as eggs is eggs, they'll come,' Cole assured him.

Before he could tell the guy to settle down, the thunder of hoofs broke the silence. A dozen riders broke cover and came dashing at full pelt into the camp. Guns blasted at the fake sleeping cowpokes. Vibrant shouts of exhilaration echoed around the site. The bloodlust of the invaders was up. Nothing was going to stop them now. The noise of exploding bullets and pounding hoofs shook the ground.

Then a cry rang out from the shadowy milieu around the edge of the camp. 'OK boys, let them have it! And make every shot count.'

Suddenly the tide had turned against the invaders. Confusion gripped Santee and his men. Hidden amongst the surrounding rocks, the defenders had them at their mercy. But no quarter was being given. Two bodies bit the dust in quick succession before Santee cottoned to the fact he had ridden into a well-prepared trap. He had seriously underestimated his old partner's ingenuity. Some of his men managed to crawl behind what limited cover was available and returned fire.

But the writing was on the wall. 'It's a trap, boys, let's get out of here while we can.' Cole instantly recognized the brusque holler from Waco Santee above the roar of battle. But escape was easier said than done. The defenders were holding the high ground that guarded the narrow entrance to the canyon. Their only defence was the darkness and the smoke issuing from gun barrels.

'Over there! They're trying to outflank us.' The cry from Idaho Blue saw a flurry of rifle shots driving the fugitives back.

Hunkered down behind some boulders, Dan Mather was sweating buckets. He knew that surrender was out of the question. By deserting his post, the ignoble foreman had waved the right to any clemency being offered. His old pals would chop him down without a moment's thought. There was only one option left. Instant flight.

If he could work his way back towards the main valley without being spotted he stood a good chance of surviving this catastrophe. Leading his horse around the hazy edges beyond the firelight, he left the other knuckleheads to their fate. And he almost made it to safety. But Mather had overlooked the very reason he had abandoned the drive in the first place.

Cole had been keeping a close eye on the Judas deserter. He had spotted the familiar figure right from the start. And now he could make his move to confront the jasper once and for all. He voiced his decision to Ed Clifford. 'Mather is trying to scuttle away.' He pointed a finger over to the vague outline moving in the shadows on the far side of the combat zone. 'I'm going after him. You keep these rats busy. I'll try to bring him back in one piece, but I ain't

147

making promises.'

'Do what you have to, son,' Clifford averred. 'Me and the boys will mop this lot up. I ain't felt so alive since the war.' The old guy was actually enjoying all the action. His .36 Cooper barked as if to express the guy's exhilaration. He even stood up to obtain a better shot at his target.

And that was his undoing. Exposed, he was at the mercy of hardened gunslingers. Two bullets struck him in the arm and shoulder. He dropped the gun and fell back. Cole cursed the guy's exuberance. There was no time to tend the wounded man if'n he wanted to catch Mather before he escaped. Eleanor was close by and quickly took control. 'You go after that traitor,' she insisted when he hesitated. 'I'll see to Dad.'

Cole nodded. Luckily the moon had just slid out from behind a bank of clouds providing enough light to track the fugitive without himself being eyeballed. There was only one way out of the canyon and Cole had a head start due to Mather's wide looping detour to avoid detection. He secreted himself on a rocky ledge and waited for the varmint to pass by underneath. Moonlight bathed the landscape in a silvery glow that would have been mesmeric in any other circumstances.

Five minutes slid by before the soft footfall reached his ears. The dark outline of a man and horse on the run emerged from the gloom. Cole timed his dive to perfection just as the rider passed beneath his lofty perch. An outstretched arm dragged the unsuspecting victim off his horse, which skittered away in panic.

On his feet in a moment, Cole powered a straight right at the guy's chin. It was a solid connection. Mather grunted under the impact, staggering back and tripping over a fallen branch.

But he was not finished yet. Desperation now drove him to seek any means to secure his escape from justice. His hand found a rock, which he hurled at the object of his wrath. Cole tried to fend it off with his left arm. The pain was excruciating and he only managed to deflect it against his head. The brutal strike was enough to stun him, delivering Mather the ascendency he needed.

The defector's laugh was more an angry snarl as he lumbered to his feet. 'This is where I finish you off once and for all,' he growled out, raising his revolver. 'And this time I won't miss.' Cole was completely at the guy's mercy. There was little of that displayed on the stony face.

The cocked weapon swung to propel its lethal charge. The gun blasted. But the detonation did not originate from Mather's revolver. A large splash of red appeared on his back as he pitched forward onto his face. Groggy and still not thinking straight, Cole managed to lumber to his feet. A familiar voice from the other side of the constricted passage soon made him realize that he was still alive and it was Dan Mather who had cashed in his chips.

'As a rule I don't cotton to shooting fellas in the back,' his saviour declared, stepping out from behind some rocks. 'But in that skunk's case I was prepared to make an exception.' Nevertheless, Waco Santee

149

kept his revolver aimed at Cole's chest. 'Now hand over that shiny six-shooter, buddy. I always fancied a nickel-plated model. In all the excitement during our last meeting, I forgot to relieve you of it. Guess I must be getting old.'

Cole placed a hand over the bleeding rent in his head, but did as ordered. 'Don't think just 'cos you saved my life, we're even. I still intend pushing this herd to Fort Belvedere. Then I'm going back to Red Mesa to pay off that loan in full.' He held the other man's gaze. 'I sincerely hope you won't stand in my way, old buddy.'

'Randle still owes me three grand for taking you out,' Santee replied. 'I'm prepared to be real generous and forego that dough if'n you keep riding.'

Cole's eyes widened. 'That mean-assed skinflint sure upped the ante. He was offering me less than half that. One more beef I have against the rat.'

'Guess we'll be having another reunion after all then,' Waco sighed. 'I sure don't want to kill you. But there might not be any choice.'

'You return my gun and we can settle this right now, man to man,' Cole suggested, leaning on a large boulder to prevent himself falling down. He was feeling distinctly light headed.

Waco shook his head. 'I never kick a man when he's down. Way you are at the moment, it would be cold-blooded murder.' And with that he mounted up, adding one final corollary. 'That's the second time in as many minutes that I've let you off'n the hook. It's getting to be a bad habit of mine. And it's the third time as I recall. So you're right. We really are well and truly even now.'

Cole attempted to focus blurry eyes on the speaker. 'You talking about the time Browny Jacobs was all set to gun me from behind?'

'You got it in one, pal. No more favours asked or given when next we meet up.' And with that stark challenge ringing across the bleak landscape, he disappeared into the darkness.

Cole untied his bandanna and held it against the bleeding cut on his head. 'None at all, old buddy,' he muttered through grating teeth. 'There'll be a showdown. You can count on it.'

His return to the campsite was at a much slower pace. But at least all the shooting had finished. Bodies were littered around the fake sleepers. Three of the attackers had been rounded up unharmed; the others were all dead. The survivors were quickly tethered and left to stew on their fate while Cole's injury was fixed up by Jumble. He would much prefer to have enjoyed the tender ministrations of Eleanor Clifford. But she insisted that her father's wound was more serious and needful of undivided attention.

FIFTEEN

DOUBLE PAY OFF

The dead bodies littering the campsite did not make for an edifying spectacle when they awoke next morning. The smell of death still hung in the air. Cole had barely slept a wink. Over a cup of strong coffee and a bacon sandwich, his first thought was for Ed Clifford.

With the wound to his own head efficiently taken care of by the versatile cook, Cole felt well enough to resume his regular duties. Ed on the other hand having had two bullets dug out of him was forced to recuperate in the wagon. A mass burial of the corpses by their surviving comrades was supervised by Red Stiller. Hangdog expressions coated the faces of the gravediggers when the grim task was completed.

'I'm letting you guys off'n the hook,' Cole magnanimously declared, assuming his most macabre look. 'But I ever see your ugly mugs again, you'll be joining them skunks in Hell.' He slung a thumb towards the line of humps. So grateful were the three men, they almost grovelled with gratitude at his feet. 'Now mount up and skedaddle afore I change my mind.' The riders did not need a second bidding.

'Sure you've done the right thing?' Clifford grunted sceptically.

'I've come across guys like that on numerous occasions before.' He gave a nod of certainty. 'Rest assured, we won't be seeing them again.'

And so around midday the drive was able to resume its trek to Fort Belvedere. Luckily it was all downhill from there on. But time was still not on their side. Luck had played a great part in the dicey enterprise so far. Very few steers had been lost. Regular scouting ahead had certainly been a significant factor in determining a feasible route to follow.

One positive element to emerge from the all-or-nothing shoot-out in the box canyon was that the crew had been thoroughly fired up, inspired by their defeat of the enemy sent against them. No grumbling about early morning calls or extra night watches. Indeed, volunteers avidly competed with one another to achieve the most. Such was their eagerness to support the two people in charge, neither of whom was back to full fitness.

Although his arm and shoulder were in a sling, Ed Clifford still wanted to get back in the saddle. But his daughter insisted that he stay put. Forced to cool his heels riding on the chuck wagon, at least the hilarious anecdotes related by Jumble about his days on

153

many a cattle drive helped while away the time.

Much as he wanted to press ahead, Cole maintained a steady pace over the next few days. Not only he and Clifford had sustained injuries. It was, therefore, with great relief that the plains on the far side of the Spruce Mountains were finally gained two weeks after the prairie blaze in the Uncompagre. Now back to full strength, the crew were able to push the herd faster.

With only one day to spare before the contract deadline expired, the wood palisade encircling Fort Belvedere finally hove into view. It had been touch and go but they had made it on time. According to the agreement signed by Dan Mather on behalf of the Flying C, each day lost would have merited a substantially reduced payout. As it was, they received the full payment from a grateful commander of the army post whose men had been living on rabbit stew and beans for the last two weeks.

'If you can guarantee to repeat this delivery every three months,' Colonel Marchbanks declared over a celebratory glass of champagne, 'I will include an extra bonus above the agreed fee.'

Cole shook hands with the army officer. 'In future I'll take the longer route around the mountains. It's a deal safer and less taxing on the heart.'

The colonel allocated rooms for them at the visitor's centre where a couple of days were needed to recover from the arduous trek. The crew were paid off which included the extra bonus and told to report back to the ranch in a week's time. With Cole's good

154

wishes and much bonhomie exuded by all, they grav-
itated to the nearest saloon for a well-earned shindig.

Over dinner that night, Cole handed the ranch
deed over to Ed Clifford. 'I have some business that
needs finishing in Red Mesa,' he intoned, a frosty
regard boding ill for the recipient as he sipped his
coffee. 'If by chance I don't return to the ranch in a
week, it reverts back you. I've written a signed affi-
davit to that effect.' He handed over an envelope.
And also if'n you're in agreement, I'd like us to
become equal partners.'

The old rancher was stunned by this offer. It was
his daughter who sealed the covenant. 'Include me in
the deal and we're in business.' What more was there
to say except to raise a special toast to the new enterprise? Although Clifford was quick to point out that
everything hung on Cole returning from his mission
safe and sound.

'Guess you don't need me telling you to watch your
step,' the old rancher warned, resting a comradely
hand on the younger man's shoulder. 'Dealing with
Kez Randle is like trying to tame a sidewinder.'

'It ain't only Randle that I'm bothered about.'

'If'n you need some back-up, I'm willing to lend
my gun arm,' the old rancher propounded flexing his
muscles, still rather stiff from the bullet wounds.

Cole suppressed a smile recalling their initial
meeting on the main street of Red Mesa. Barely a
month since, yet it seemed more like a year. 'Much
obliged for the offer, Ed. But this is something I have
to do alone.'

Clifford nodded his understanding. 'But there's one person you do need to heed.' He pushed back his chair and stood up heading for the door as Eleanor hurried across from where she had been choosing a dessert of pecan pie and fresh cream. She couldn't help but overhear the grim declaration.

'I know that it's futile trying to persuade you otherwise,' she murmured in that husky low drawl that set his heart a pounding. 'But I don't want to be helping Dad run the Flying C on my own. We're all in this together. And that's how I want it to stay.' She sat down and kissed him on the cheek, her lips lingering with an unspoken message that almost made him revoke the promise of revenge.

Almost, but not quite. Gently he pushed her away and stood up. There were some things that a man could not walk around. A prolonged, drawn-out look of aspiring ardour passed between them. Moments later Cole Jardine, once again the infamous Kingpin, had disappeared into the night. Tears dribbled down the girl's cheeks. Had he lived, Dan Mather would have been consumed by jealousy.

Her father sympathized, offering an optimistic outcome that had no effect on his distraught daughter. 'Don't worry, honey. Cole knows how to take care of himself. Likely he'll be back at the ranch before us.'

The man in question had set himself a direct course following the trail over which they had brought the cattle. On this occasion he made much better time, arriving back at Red Mesa four days later.

Sleeping in the saddle had become second nature to him. He drew to a halt on the edge of town, working out in his mind how best to tackle the finale of the bizarre adventure into which he had been pitched.

The direct approach seemed like the best option. He tied up outside the Yellow Dog and pushed open the batwings. The place was heavy with a mixture of burning tallow and cigar smoke, which hung in the air like a curtain. A dozen drinkers stood at the bar. Nobody noticed the newcomer as he made a beeline for the stairs at the far end.

That was when a blunt-edged voice cut through the general hubbub.

'Can't let you do it, Cole,' his old partner snapped out. 'Randle still wants you dead. And he won't pay up until you're lying on the undertaker's slab.'

Lily Devine tried to pull him away. 'Don't!' she hissed in his ear. 'He's your oldest friend.' Santee pushed her away. 'Keep out of this, Lily. It's between me and him. Us going up against each other was always on the cards. Now it's arrived, I ain't backing down.'

The only sign that Cole had heard the curt warning was a slight stiffening of the shoulders. His pace faltered not a jot as he made to climb the stairs. 'One last chance, buddy. You know I ain't for back-shooting but I will if needs must.'

Men quickly sobered up seeing that a gunfight was about to erupt in their midst. As one, those at the bar moved out of the line of fire.

On hearing the palaver inside the saloon, Kez

Randle chose that moment to appear at a door adjacent to the bar where he had been packing essentials into a carpet bag ready for quitting Red Mesa. He had already emptied the safe. His horse was saddled up out back.

Ever since Santee had returned alone from the failed ambush, the unscrupulous land grabber had known that the game was up. Sooner or later Cole Jardine would arrive. And there would be only one thing on his mind, a bullet with Kez Randle's name on it. Santee had assured him that he never walked away from an unfinished job. But Randle knew they went back aways and didn't trust him to deliver. Now Jardine was here.

He hadn't spotted Santee standing at the far end of the bar. All he could see was the back of the man who had destroyed all his plans. He drew a Marston three shot pocket pistol from inside his coat. He couldn't miss at this range; then all his problems would be solved.

Gunfire rattled the windows. But it was Kez Randle who staggered forward, arms flailing wildly before he fell to floor. Smoke dribbled from Santee's Colt .45, the one he had appropriated from his friend. 'Nicely balanced but pulls a bit to the left,' he remarked nonchalantly as Cole swung on his heel, drawing his own borrowed revolver. 'Reckon I'll stick with the Remington.'

Cole's eyes widened on seeing the gambler lying in a pool of his own blood. His gaze shifted to the man who had killed him, now pushing the Peacemaker along the bar. In its place he filled his hand with a glass of whiskey.

Slowly ambling back down the stairs, Cole followed suit. 'I thought you were the one who wanted to see which of us was the faster,' he said sidling up to his pal who had been rejoined by the much-relieved singer.

'Reckon I lost interest all of sudden. This calls for another drink. Set 'em up for everyone, bartender. My buddy here is paying. I'm getting a mite tired of saving his hide.' Cole could only shrug, conceding the assertion had some truth in it.

There were many more drinks to follow over the next couple of days, the two hired guns promising never again to work on opposite sides of the fence. On the third day after they had sobered up and enjoyed a good breakfast, Cole was ready to head back to the Flying C. 'Reckon I've found where I belong,' he told his pal. 'No more hiring out to skunks like Randle. And if'n you've a mind to follow a similar trail, the spread next to mine is up for sale at a knock-down price. Randle won't be needing the land anymore.' The notion caused them both much hilarity.

Waco mused on the notion. 'Sounds like a good idea. Figure I'm about ready to hang up my guns as well. That dough we found in Randle's saddle-bag, plus a little extra for all the trouble he's caused will set me up fine.' A frown of uncertainty clouded his bristly features. 'But it all depends on whether Lily is willing to join me.'

159

'You try and stop me, big fella,' was the crisp endorsement of the suggestion from the lady in question, who had just walked into the diner. 'I'm done with all that warbling and sashaying around for lecherous guys to lust over. From here on I'm a one-man gal.' And she plonked herself on Waco's knee and kissed him on the lips, much to the amusement of the diner's clientele who applauded vigorously.

Waco responded with passion. Having surfaced from the clinch, he gasped out, 'Then it looks like I'm gonna be in the ranching business as well, and we're gonna be neighbours.'

'All that's left for me to do,' Cole mused thoughtfully, 'is to make sure Elly is of a like mind.'

Lily had the final say. 'Reckon there's gonna be a double wedding in Red Mesa this fall, folks. And you're all invited.' More cheering from the assembled crowd. Everybody loves a celebration.